"I'd like you to come for supper tomorrow…"

With only three days left before Martha was scheduled to leave, she and Paul were well aware of their upcoming separation and what it might mean for their budding relationship. Paul said he'd try to come for a visit after she was back home a couple of weeks.

"So, you've told your family about me?"

"Not everything," Paul said with a crooked smile, "but they know I'm not home much and they suspected it was a woman."

Martha grinned. "The word *woman* makes me feel so old."

"You're twenty. That makes you a woman."

"Still…"

"I really care for you a lot."

"I know. Me, too."

Her heart began beating wildly. Hopefully, her heart would remain in place and he wouldn't be aware of her nervousness. The moment was over in an instant, but somehow, it changed the equation entirely. They were no longer just friends.

A line had been crossed.

June Bryan Belfie has written over twenty-five novels. Her Amish books have been bestsellers and have sold around the world. She lives in Pennsylvania and is familiar with the ways of her Amish neighbors. Mother of five and grandmother of eight, Ms. Belfie enjoys writing clean and wholesome stories for people of all ages.

AN AMISH SECRET

June Bryan Belfie

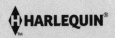

Recycling programs
for this product may
not exist in your area.

ISBN-13: 978-1-335-49966-0

An Amish Secret

Copyright © 2017 by June Bryan Belfie

This edition published by arrangement with Harlequin Books S.A.

For questions and comments about the quality of this book, please contact us at CustomerService@Harlequin.com.

Printed in U.S.A.

Chapter One

Sarah Troyer rubbed her sore hip as she straightened her posture and walked away from the huge water-bath canner filled with fresh tomato puree. It was a busy time for an Amish woman as the garden produced the vegetables to be processed for the winter.

It would have been easier if her daughter Martha had not decided to visit Sarah's elder sister outside of Soudersburg. Though it was only a little over a mile from their farm outside of Paradise, it still took a few minutes by buggy, especially since the tourist season was still in full swing. *Jah*, she sure wished she'd stayed home today to help her.

Sarah's sister Lizzy was nearly sixty and had been blessed with a large family, though she had all boys—eight altogether. Her one daughter had been stillborn. A difficult time. Lizzy had been comforted only by the attention she received from her niece, little Martha, who was only a toddler at the time Lizzy suffered her loss. Their affection for each other was deep and sometimes caused jealous thoughts to enter Sarah's mind and heart.

Jealousy was an unwelcome visitor, which she quickly forced out through prayer.

There would still be more canning to do when Martha did return. It seemed there was always more to do. Since it was just the three of them, Sarah often shared her pantry items with her family members. It gave her great pleasure to stock her mother's cupboard in the *dawdi-haus* next door, since her dear mother found it difficult to do much in the kitchen with the arthritis in her hands. Somehow, she was still able to quilt upon occasion, though her stitches were longer than and not as even as they once were.

Sarah's husband, Melvin, came in through the kitchen door and smiled over at his wife, who had poured herself a second cup of coffee. "Any *kaffi* left for your husband?" he asked.

"Oh *jah*, I made twelve cups this morning. I'll get you some." She began to rise and he held up his hand.

"*Nee*, I'll get my own. You work too hard as it is. Where's that *dochder* of ours?"

"Martha went over to Lizzy's to help her with painting the sitting room. She's holding church in two weeks."

"I would think with eight *sohns*, your *schwester* wouldn't need our Martha."

"Well, you know they love to work together."

"Her place is with you, Sarah. I'll have a talk with her this evening. I've noticed you walk with a limp lately."

"Oh, not too bad. I'll try not to walk that way."

"It shows you're straining yourself is all. You ain't as young as you used to be."

"*Nee*? Well, mercy me, here I thought I was getting younger," she quipped.

Melvin grinned over as he poured himself a full mug

of rich dark coffee and took a seat adjacent to his wife. After a sip, he set the mug down. "Any sticky buns left?"

"You ate the last one at breakfast. I need to start the dough for more."

"Don't you bother. You still have molasses cookies left. I know. I checked this morning."

"You sure have a sweet tooth," she said with a chuckle. "Me, too. I wish I could lose a few pounds."

"Don't you worry about a couple extra pounds. It's just more to love." He patted her hand. "Can't believe we've been married thirty-one years already."

"I was pretty young, wasn't I? Only eighteen."

"Prettiest *maed* in the district."

"Oh," she said with a blush. "You just say that."

"It's true. I had to work hard to get you to notice me."

"Mmm. I always knew when you were around. I thought you were the nicest *bu* in the crowd. I'm sorry we didn't have the large family you wanted." She lowered her eyes and moved her hand away to stir more sugar into her mug.

"Well, at least I have you. I was pretty scared I might lose you when they said you had cancer."

"*Jah*, it was a scary time. I guess it was *gut* they caught it early. But I sure didn't like having my womb removed at nineteen."

"It's okay, honey. You know *Gott* brought us Martha to help the emptiness we were feeling."

"*Jah*, thank *Gott* for that. I suppose we need to tell her someday that she's adopted."

"It don't matter none," Melvin said. "We couldn't love her anymore if she was from our own bodies."

"That's true. Besides, the subject just never came up."

"Moving here from Ohio was probably a *gut* idea. That way there were no questions to answer."

"That was a *Gott* thing, too. Inheriting this acreage from your *dawdi* sure helped out," Sarah reminded him.

"*Jah*, since I was one of ten, there sure wouldn't have been much of my *daed's* land left for me. So you see, everything works out for those who trust. When I'm done here, I need to check Millie."

"What's wrong with her? She's always been a good milker."

"*Jah*, she has, but just like the rest of us, age is catching up with her. Do you know she's more than ten years old now?"

Sarah nodded. "*Jah*, and she's given us a dozen calves. She's earned her keep."

"She's not producing as much lately and she looked sore. I want to put ointment on her."

"You're a *gut* man. Always looking for ways to be kind. I'm glad I said yes to you."

After he left the kitchen, Sarah checked the clock and then turned off the canning pot and slowly removed the hot jars when it was time. As she pulled out the last quart of the bright colored tomato puree, she heard the door and turned to see Martha come in. She had a paper bag in her hand.

"*Hallo*, Martha. What's in the *toot*?" Sarah asked her daughter.

"*Aenti* Lizzy had extra pretzels, so she wanted you to have them."

"Oh, she makes the best. Did you finish the painting?"

"Almost. I hope to go back tomorrow to help her finish, if it's okay with you."

"I guess." A frown spread across her face.

"Guess? Would you rather I stay home to help you, *Mamm*?"

"It's okay. I wanted to do beans tomorrow, but I can handle it alone."

"I'll only stay about two hours and then we can work on the beans together. She just needs it finished so she can get the floor buffed up a little before the church service."

"*Jah*, that's fine. My back's been acting up a bit, or I wouldn't even mention it."

"Oh, I'm so sorry." Martha went over to her mother and kissed her cheek. "I'll leave early so I can be home by noon. And I'll stay home the rest of the week, I promise."

"You're a *gut maed*, Martha. I don't know what I'd do without you."

"Well, hopefully you won't have to find out for a long time. If I marry Daniel Beiler, we'll be right up the road. A hop, skip and a jump!"

"That would be ever so nice. Has he asked you yet?"

"Kind of. We've talked about things, you know. Like how many *kinner* we want and what foods he loves the most…"

"So you're twenty now. I guess you're ready."

"That's one reason I want to take my kneeling vows within a year, so I'll be ready. Daniel already took his."

"*Jah*, I remember. Guess we better tell *Daed* not to get rid of the celery at the stand."

Martha giggled as she placed her sweater on a peg and washed her hands. "What are we having for supper? Can I make anything?"

"Just the leftover pot roast from yesterday. There're

still lots of vegetables left in it. I did make tapioca pudding this morning, though."

"Oh yum! I'll need all your recipes, *Mamm*, when I do marry. I'll never cook as *gut* as you do, but at least I can try."

"Already you make better brownies than I do, Martha. Even *Daed* says so."

"He just wants me to feel *gut*."

"*Nee*, he's a truthful man. He wouldn't do just flattery."

"Well, I guess Daniel and I can eat brownies for breakfast," Martha said, grinning.

"Now that would suit your *daed* just perfect," Sarah said, nodding. When she smiled broadly, her dimples were accentuated. She was a pretty woman nearing fifty and her extra weight did not detract. The family loved her exactly as she was.

Being part of this Amish community was one of Sarah's greatest joys. Even though she only had the one child, she didn't have enough fingers to count all those who loved her and went out of their way to be with her. *Jah*, the Amish way was her way, for sure and for certain.

Chapter Two

The next day, Martha rinsed out the paintbrushes in the pot sink in her aunt's basement as Lizzy busied herself picking up the plastic sheets protecting the pine wood floors in the old farmhouse's main sitting room.

Martha checked her watch and it was only eleven o'clock. They finished ahead of schedule and she was anxious to return home to help her mother with the canning. She'd really looked tired the day before. It was important to lend a hand with all the chores at this time of year.

So many vegetables were ready for preserving and it was too much work for one person. Several of her mother's nieces came by occasionally to help out, but most of them had large families of their own and really needed to work on their own projects. Good thing Martha planned to live nearby once she married. Would it be this fall? She wouldn't mind pushing it a bit.

If she were going to have a large family, it would be ever so nice to start right away. How happy it would make her parents to have lots of grandchildren to spoil since they'd only had her. She never talked to her mother about being the only child. She feared it would upset her mother to talk about it since she saw her tear up once when her mother had held one of her niece's new babies.

When she arrived in the kitchen, Lizzy was putting a kettle on for tea.

"I really should get home, *Aenti*. *Mamm* needs my help."

"Oh, surely you have time for one cup of tea. I made your special crumb cake last night so you could have a nice big piece today. And then I'll wrap some up for your folks. Tell that *schwester* of mine that she's been scarce lately. I miss her dropping in. She should have come by today with you. I wouldn't expect her to paint, if she didn't reckon to. Like me, I know her arthritis gives her a hard time sometimes."

"*Jah*, that it does. We'll try to stop by next week sometime. I know she's thinking the corn will be ready early so maybe we can put some up together."

"*Jah*, sounds like fun. Ours is popping up early this year. All that rain and sunshine we've been getting, I guess. The Lord is doing *gut* on giving us just the right amount of everything this year."

"That's what *Daed* said last night. I'll stay a couple minutes. I sure love your crumb cake. I'll need your recipe soon, *Aenti*."

"Oh?" Lizzy looked over at her niece as she removed the foil from the top of the pan with the crumb cake. "Are you trying to tell me something, young lady?"

Martha laughed. "I'm not saying a word—yet. Just thinking ahead is all."

"It's that young Daniel Beiler, *jah*? The nice-looking boy with the green eyes?"

"Now how would you know that?" Martha asked as

she took down two cups from the cupboard and set them on the long kitchen table.

Lizzy reached for her favorite yellow teapot and added three teabags as she grinned back. "I see how he smiles at you. Reminds me of your *Onkel* Leroy before he courted me. Always smiling and winking. Thought he had a tic for a while."

"Well, I have to admit, Daniel is someone I could be interested in. In fact, I may as well confess. I am. We see each other every week, but don't tell anyone. It's a secret and besides, it's not official yet. He hasn't really asked me."

"Well now, that does make a difference. He'd be crazy if he doesn't ask—and soon. You ain't gonna be single long, missy, not with that lovely dark hair and that little dimple in your chin."

"Now don't make me proud, *Aenti*. I'm an Amish *maed*, after all."

"I won't say another word. Now let me check the water and get a knife for the cake. I suspect we'll see your *onkel* before long. It's nearly time for him to take a break."

Sarah checked out the front window. It was nearly noon, and Martha was due home. Good thing, since her back was aching something fierce. Melvin had picked a bushel of string beans that needed to be prepared for the winter and until she had help, they'd have to sit and wait.

Now, her sister knew she couldn't do it all herself. She should have thought of someone beside herself for once. She was like that as a girl, too—always putting her needs ahead of everyone else's. How many times had Sarah ended up cleaning the kitchen after supper without her sister's help, just so Lizzy could run off with friends?

Ach. Their mother had sure spoiled her, that was for certain, and even now, Leroy catered to his wife. And of course, the eight boys and their wives treated her like she was someone special. If they didn't, Lizzy would pout and make everyone miserable, just like she did when she was a teenager.

Sarah wondered if anyone else noticed it. She daresn't bring up the subject with her mother. She had started to say something once, and the look on her mother's face took the subject right off the table. Her *mamm* prided herself on treating each of her children the same, though everyone in the family knew that Lizzy and their eldest brother, Tobias, were the apples of her mother's eye.

The little green devil was cropping up again and Sarah berated herself as she turned back to the kitchen and filled the sink with cold water as she pulled the basket of beans closer to the sink. She might as well get started. They weren't going to can themselves—that was for sure.

Around quarter of twelve, Sarah heard the crushing of stones on the driveway as Martha returned in the family buggy. All was forgotten as she saw her daughter walk towards the house with a large plateful of crumb cake covered in clear wrap.

"Wow, look at that. Now why can't I make crumb cake as *gut* as my *schwester*?" she asked as she held the door open for her daughter.

"But you make the best lemon sponge cake, that's for sure," Martha said as she laid the plate down and went to wash her hands in the other side of the sink. "I see you're getting ready with the beans. Why don't you sit with *Daed* and have the cake while I wash these up? He called out from the barn that he'd be in for a break after he puts Chessy out to pasture."

"I don't mind if I do. I'll put fresh *kaffi* on. Do you want some too?"

"*Nee, danki.* I had tea with *Aenti* Lizzy when we were done painting. I'm full as can be."

"Oh. That's nice." Sarah turned her head so Martha wouldn't notice her disappointment.

"And she wants to get together soon. She said she misses you."

"I doubt that."

Martha looked over, arching her brows. "Why wouldn't she mean it?"

"Oh, you wouldn't understand. I suppose we can stop by for a while after we get the food put up. We have the corn coming up soon."

"We thought it would be fun to put it up together."

"She said that?"

"*Jah. Mamm*, you sound funny. What's wrong?"

"Nothing at all. Just don't feel so *gut* today. I guess I'm a little out of sorts. Ignore me, Martha. I'll get over it. Maybe the crumb cake will help." She brought two plates to the table and a couple of forks and then went over to make a fresh pot of coffee. As it was perking, Melvin came in and washed up.

"I sure need *kaffi* today. Didn't sleep *gut* last night."

"I heard you tossing about. What was wrong?" Sarah asked her husband.

"Don't know. Just couldn't settle down. Maybe a mugful of brew will help."

Martha worked on the beans as her parents sat and chatted. The weather had cooled considerably and even with the stove going for the beans, it was pleasant in the stark white kitchen, decorated with only a calendar of farm scenes and the old pine family wall clock, which had been in their family for three generations.

Once the women were done for the day, Martha went next door to visit her grandparents while her mother went upstairs to lie down for a rest.

Martha loved her *mammi* and *dawdi*. They were pleased when she paid them a visit and often she'd insist on making a pot of soup or stew for them while she was there, which they accepted willingly. When she had more than an hour to give, she'd help her grandmother mend clothing or run a wash for her down in the basement. It was too late in the day to start a wash, but she folded towels and sheets which her grandmother had brought in from the line earlier in the day.

Her grandfather had injured one of his legs in a farming accident years before and had to get around with a walker. He was one of the deacons for the church district and spent time visiting members of the congregation, which relieved his wife, who confided in Martha once that when they were together too constantly, she had little time to quilt, which was one of her joys. She encouraged his visiting the parishioners and he saw her willingness to part with his presence as an act of spiritual dedication on her part. It worked out well all the way around.

"I want to take you shopping one day, Martha," she said as her granddaughter stirred carrots into the venison stew. "You can pick out the fabrics for the next quilt I want to work on. It will be for your wedding someday."

"Seriously? How wonderful," Martha said, delighted with the idea. "Do I get to pick the pattern too?"

"Sure, if it ain't too hard. I was thinking about the double wedding ring."

"I love that one, but let me think about it first. This is so exciting. Did you tell *Mamm* yet? Does she want to help?"

"I'm sure she will, but I hate to say it, your *mamm* don't sew as *gut* as she used to, so I won't push it. Her stitches are even longer than mine."

"If she wants to though, please let her. I don't mind if the stitches aren't perfect. It would be nice to know she helped, if you know what I mean."

"Oh, true. I hadn't thought of that. Of course, I'll ask her to help when the time comes."

"Maybe you can come along when I need to go to market for *Mamm*. We can stop at the fabric store in Soudersburg."

"We can pick up your *Aenti* Lizzy first and she can help you pick out the colors. She has a *gut* eye for patterns."

"That would be fun! Maybe *Mamm* will go, too."

"We can ask her, though she's not as *gut* planning quilts as her *schwester*."

"She knits wonderful-*gut* though. At least she used to."

"*Jah*, I still have the first sweater she made for me."

After Martha left the *dawdi-haus*, she heard a buggy approach. When she looked up, she saw it was Daniel Beiler, just in time for supper. He always managed to come by when there was food headed for the table. *Jah*, he was probably the one. She never remembered feeling this way about any other young man. She waved and stood waiting for him to tether the horse. Hopefully, he'd stay all evening and maybe he'd even ask the question.

Chapter Three

After he secured his buggy to their hitching post, Daniel came over to her, and then without touching, they walked towards the kitchen door.

"I see you managed to get here in time for supper," she said, grinning over at him.

"Your *mamm* is a better cook than mine."

"Ooo, naughty *bu*. You'll have to pay me to keep that one to myself."

"Let me think what it's worth. Maybe you'll accept a kiss later."

"Oh, how proud our Amishman is today. That one's not going to work."

He reached for the door handle and waited for her to enter before he did. She stepped in as her mother turned from the stove.

"*Hallo*, Daniel. I wondered if that was you coming by. Can you stay for supper? Just having leftover barley soup with pumpernickel bread tonight."

"Sounds *gut. Danki.*"

"Martha, set another place for Daniel and cut up the bread, if you will. I'll ring the bell for your *daed*."

"I'll do it," Daniel offered.

"Well isn't that thoughtful? *Danki*."

Within ten minutes the four of them were seated around the table and they lowered their heads for the silent blessing of the food. Melvin cleared his throat when he was done and Martha rose to serve up the soup. No one spoke as they attended to their meal. The bread was passed around more than once. Then as Martha cleared the soup bowls, Sarah prepared the clear glass dessert dishes with mounds of cinnamon-flavored bread pudding for each of them.

"Does anyone want *kaffi* with dessert?" Sarah asked. The men nodded, so Martha prepared a pot and set it upon the stove.

Sarah placed the largest bowlful of dessert in front of her guest and he smiled in appreciation.

"You make the very best bread pudding," he said.

"*Jah*? I'll make sure Martha gets my recipe," she said without considering her words.

There was silence and Martha lowered her head as a flush ran up her neck. After all, he hadn't actually proposed yet. Oh, my.

Realizing her snafu, Sarah quickly changed the subject and asked about Daniel's crops. He seemed a bit relieved and avoided looking at Martha, who concentrated on her dessert. Melvin was oblivious to the entire thing. He sat back and pulled on his beard, nodding as Daniel described the wonderful growth of his corn.

After they ate, Daniel followed Melvin out to the barn while Sarah and Martha *redded* up the kitchen.

"*Mamm*, why would you say that about the recipe?

You know he hasn't officially asked me yet. He may not be planning to at this point."

"I realized too late. *Es dutt mir leed. Jah*, I'm real sorry."

Martha laid her sponge aside and patted her mother's shoulder. "It's okay. Maybe he didn't notice."

"I'm afraid he did, but really, why would he be here so often, if he wasn't smitten with you, *dochder*?"

"He likes your food. He told me himself. It's better than his *mudder*'s."

"That's a new one," she said with a chuckle. "Now, you go see your friend and I'll finish up scouring the sink."

"*Danki*." Martha laid her damp apron aside for a fresh one, and headed out the door. She found her father and Daniel in the corner of the dairy barn, speaking in soft tones. She wondered if they were discussing her and even thought of turning around to avoid interrupting their conversation, but Daniel looked up and nodded.

"Hi, Martha. Your *daed* was just telling me about Millie. She's much better."

Her father, who had his back towards her, turned and nodded. "*Jah*, we'll be keeping the gal a while longer, that's for sure. I'm going in now. You two can have the barn to yourselves."

Now what on earth did he have in mind? Martha stayed by the entrance instead. "I thought we'd take a walk now, *Daed*. It's a nice evening."

"*Jah*, that it is. *Gut* idea. I'd join you, but I want to read. Don't forget devotions in half an hour. You're welcome to join us, Daniel."

"*Danki*, but my parents will be expecting me. *Daed*'s

eyes aren't *gut*. He needs glasses, I'm afraid, so he wants me to read to the others tonight."

"Oh, *jah*, I had to get glasses last year myself. Ain't fun, but the ones at the drug store worked out real *gut*. Tell him to go there first."

"*Jah*, I will."

As Melvin walked down the path to the house, Martha and Daniel headed over to the horse pasture where the work horses were grazing along with their beautiful chestnut Arabian driving horse. They were out of sight of the farmhouse and Daniel reached for Martha's hand. "You look nice tonight."

"*Jah*? So other nights I don't?"

"I didn't say that," he said, pouting slightly.

"Just kidding, Daniel. You take me too serious-like."

"I don't know how to take you sometimes. You have a funny sense of humor."

"I'll try to be more serious."

"*Nee*, that's not what I'm saying. Oh, women." He dropped her hand and leaned on the fence. The family dog, Spunky, joined them and rubbed against Martha's skirt, looking for a comforting pat. Martha knelt beside the short-haired mutt, and rubbed behind his ears.

"You know me, don't you Spunky. Dogs seem to understand better than people sometimes."

"*Jah*. You have to understand where I come from. My family is very serious. Not a lot of laughter in our house, though we all get along okay. My *daed* rarely smiles even, so it's fun to be with your family, but sometimes, I don't know how to take things. Like your *mudder* talking about the recipe. Was she making some kind of a point? Everyone looked funny after she said it."

"Well, if you can't figure that one out, I guess you

really don't know how to take people. Don't worry about it. I guess she just wants me to be a *gut* cook like her—someday."

"I see." He knelt beside her and the dog, and Spunky turned his attention to him. "Our dog has been missing for a week now. I guess we'll have to get a new one," he said.

"Aren't you going to look for him first?"

"We did. We went around the whole place and called him, but haven't seen a trace of him. He was getting old anyway."

"You sound so…so heartless."

"I'm not heartless." His voice took on an edge. "But it's only a dog, for Pete's sake. We cared for him when he was alive. He was a good herder."

"Mmm. I'll keep my ears open for someone who has pups. I think Valerie's dog was expecting. Nice Lab."

"*Danki*. Let me know." He stood up and straightened his back. "I guess I should head for home. My *daed* doesn't like to be kept waiting."

"I'll walk you over to your buggy."

"I may not get to the Singing this week. We have family coming from Ohio and I should stay home to be with them."

"That's okay. I'll go over with a friend."

"Girlfriend?"

"Most likely."

"Hope so."

"Well, we aren't committed to each other. Yet."

"True. I have no hold over you."

"Not at this point." Now seemed like the moment—if there was to be one.

It passed. "Let's head back," he said solemnly. There

was distance larger than measurable between them. What had happened? Why was there this strain?

When they reached his buggy, he offered a slight smile. "I'll miss you. But I'll stop by once my family leaves, if that's okay."

"Sure. Of course. Have a nice time when they visit." She pushed forth the brightest smile she could muster and watched as he pulled himself up into the driver's seat and clucked at his horse, who began his journey down the lane. Usually he turned back to wave when he reached the road, but tonight he kept his eyes straight ahead.

When Martha went back into the kitchen, her mother was just heading for the sitting room. "*Gut*, your *daed* was just about to start our Bible reading. Let's join him. Is Daniel coming too?"

Martha shook her head and followed her mother into the room where her father was already sitting in his special armchair with the family Bible spread open upon his lap. The chapter from Ezekiel was one she usually enjoyed, but tonight her attention was elsewhere.

Perhaps she had imagined Daniel Beiler's interest in her. Maybe it was time to see who else was available. Her heart lay heavy in her petite chest and she asked the Lord to forgive her for not paying attention to the reading of the word. There was always comfort in the passages her father read, just knowing they were given by the great creator through his Holy Spirit to man. Tonight was an exception. Daniel wasn't the only man in the world—even though at that moment, it felt like he was.

Chapter Four

Daniel drove slowly back to his home, which was nearly a mile away from the Troyer's farm. What had happened between him and Martha tonight? Why did he feel so discouraged all at once? Surely, if she was this moody before they marry, he'd be looking for trouble to pursue their relationship much longer. He had noticed Molly Zook at church smile over several times. She was a good catch, for sure. Her parents owned more land than most, too, though that shouldn't enter into his thoughts. Her pretty blonde hair and pastel coloring made her a pleasant sight to any young man.

But Martha. He thought she was the one. She was so different from him though. Hard to put into words really. Sometimes he wondered if she was making fun of him when she pulled her quirky little remarks. In his home, it was obvious what every statement meant. There were few words exchanged between the members of his family, so each word had weight. Not frivolous conversation. Could he ever get used to Martha's sense of humor?

When he pulled into his drive, he saw three of his brothers playing catch. They nodded to him as he drove his buggy past them towards the barn. After caring for his horse, he joined them and they stepped back to make room for him. The catch lasted for only about ten minutes, when his father called for them to join him for devotions.

Silently, they placed the ball and gloves back in a storage trunk in the barn and made their way back to the house. Timothy, who was twenty-one years old was born exactly one year before Daniel. He asked why he wasn't home for supper. "*Mamm* was annoyed. She made grilled cheese sandwiches for you. They got cold."

"She knows I often stop off at a friend's to have supper. Was *Daed* upset too?"

"He didn't seem to notice. You'd better apologize to *Mamm* though or she'll give you the silent treatment for a week."

"I will."

"So, who do you go see almost every evening? A *maed*?"

"I'd rather not say."

"Okay. Whatever you want."

"Sorry, I was short with you, but it is someone I was interested in. Now I'm not so sure."

"If you want to talk about it, you know I'd be happy to listen."

"*Danki*. Not at this point."

The family sat together in the large sitting room, the younger children on pillows on the floor. They sat silently while Daniel's father began with prayer and then handed the Bible over to Daniel to read. He felt awkward at first reading in front of his whole family. His three brothers and four sisters were all younger than he was and he noticed his mother had put extra weight on in the waistline and he suspected there might be another child on the way.

He had hoped he'd be married within the next couple years so he, too, could begin a large family. Now he wasn't so sure who his choice would be. It wasn't time to give up on Martha, but nothing had been said yet to commit him, so he could certainly look around at other perspective brides. Maybe he'd find a woman he could understand. That would be ever so nice.

Three weeks passed when Sarah sat with her husband for coffee one afternoon. "I got a letter today from one of my cousins who lives near Lewistown, here in Pennsylvania. Remember my third cousin Deborah?" Sarah asked her husband.

"The one with triplets and a lazy husband?"

"*Jah*, that's the one. Anyway, she wondered if we could let Martha go visit next month to help out. She's expecting a set of twins and the other ones are only three or four."

"Ain't she got family nearby?"

"*Jah*, but apparently, some of her *schwesters* are in a family way themselves and her mother injured her back. It wouldn't be for long. Maybe a month. She tried to find a young girl to help out, but she wasn't able to come up with anyone."

"Well, you need Martha yourself."

"Oh, by then, we'll have most of the food put up. I can do the pickling. I think we should help out."

"You should ask Martha about it first."

"*Jah*, she's getting the sheets off the line. I'll talk to her when she comes in. It might be nice for her to get away for a bit. Especially since we haven't seen that Daniel for a couple weeks."

"Is that why she goes around with a long face? You'd think someone had died the way she's acting."

"I think it may be over between them. It's not easy to get over a broken heart."

"Well, it's not like they was planning a wedding now, is it?"

"I think she had hoped there'd be a proposal."

"I'm kinda glad it didn't happen. Daniel is a nice young man, but his father is a sourpuss, if you ask me." Melvin stirred cream into a fresh cup of coffee.

"*Jah*, even his wife is a gloomy person. I was in favor of it at first, but the more I think about it, the more I wonder. She ain't getting any younger though. Don't want her to end up a spinster."

"Worse things than that. My one sister is the happiest one in the family and she never even went out with a man."

Sarah laughed. "Maybe she has the right idea. Here comes Martha. I'll run it by her about visiting Deborah."

Martha came in carrying a large wicker laundry basket. She had folded the sheets and towels carefully as she laid them back in. "They smell so *gut*. I love to hang things out this time of year."

"*Jah*, any time is *gut*, until the clothes freeze on the line," her mother added. She proceeded to tell Martha about the request from Deborah. Martha sat down at the table and rested her head on her hands after placing her elbows on the table.

"I barely know her, but sure, if she needs help and you can manage without me, I'd be happy to go. That will be quite a handful for her. Five *kinner*—all under five! Mercy!"

"Hopefully it will only be for about a month. We need to help *Daed* with the harvest this year."

"Now, I can manage alone," Melvin said.

"You know it's easier if we all chip in our time, Melvin. You admitted that to me last year. Remember?"

"I guess that's true."

"You guess? Goodness, your memory must be failing you. Getting to be an old goat, are you? May have to put you out to pasture."

"When you write back, find out the date. We'll have to hire a driver, *Mamm*," Martha said, slightly anxious about staying with people she barely knew. She couldn't even remember what the husband looked like, but she remembered Deborah as being overly thin with sparse hair tightly drawn under her *kapp*. Pleasant enough, though. It would all work out. It would be good to get away from Lancaster area for a while until she got over her disappointment in Daniel. He had stopped by one afternoon the week before, but only stayed for a few minutes, even refusing to stay for supper. It had been so strained that Martha was relieved when he made an excuse to leave. So much for love.

She knew several couples who really didn't love each other when they married. Apparently, it was a union of convenience, based on mutual respect. Their marriages appeared just as satisfactory as the ones where the couples were madly in love with each other. She could probably make the best of such an arrangement, as long as she knew the man had fine character and he was somewhat attractive to her. She wasn't at that point yet, but she did consider the possibility down the road, if she didn't find someone she cared deeply about first.

A couple weeks later, Deborah wrote back and suggested Martha head over as soon as possible since the doctor suspected she'd go into labor within days.

Martha stopped over at her friend Naomi Shoemaker's house the day before she planned to leave. They sat outside under a shady oak tree sipping sweet tea while Naomi's baby sister napped in her carriage. Martha told her about her plans to visit her cousin.

"Lucky you. I wish I could get away for a while. Sometimes I even think I'm not cut out for being Amish. Don't breathe a word of this, Martha. You're the only one I've ever said that to."

"I'm shocked! Why on earth do you feel that way?"

"I don't know. Sometimes, it seems all we do is work. I'd like to travel and wear pretty clothes once in a while. Don't you ever think about jumping the fence?"

"Once in a great while, after canning for ten days straight," she said with a grin. "But I'd miss the *gut* part of being Amish. Like having a close family and community. I'd really miss that."

"I know. So would I. I'll probably never leave. It's just nice to know I could without being banned. *Mamm* keeps pushing me to get baptized, but I'm just not ready to make a life-time commitment yet. I know you're not baptized yet, are you?"

"*Nee.*"

"You'll need to be, if you plan on marrying soon. Are you going to tell your very best friend how things are going with 'you know who'?"

"That's pretty much over with." Martha let out a long sigh.

"So that's why you weren't at the Singing together. He showed up alone."

"Who did he take home, did you notice?"

Naomi looked down at the sleeping baby and tucked the blanket on one side, without looking up. "I guess."

"You can tell me. I have a right to know. It won't devastate me, I promise."

She looked up, her lips turned down. "Are you sure?"

"Absolutely."

"Molly Zook."

"No way! She's soooo boring!"

"That's probably what he likes. You have to admit, he's not exactly a ball of fire himself."

"You noticed."

"Everybody notices. No one figured you two would get together, but you went home with him at least four times in the last few months."

"Five times. What a waste. You're right though. I had to do nearly all the talking. It did get boring sometimes. He's real cute though."

"Cute isn't enough. You have to be able to talk about stuff."

"Then maybe it's just as well it's over."

"I think so."

"Okay, I've told you my secrets. Now how about you, Naomi. Anyone you're interested in?"

"A couple guys, but so far, it hasn't been the same with them. I think that's another reason I'm discouraged."

The baby lifted her head and grunted a few times. "It's time for Patty to see her *mudder*. I'll take her in and come back to finish our tea. Then I have to do another wash. I do diapers every day. We have three in diapers right now. Wish we could use disposable."

"That will never happen. It's not good for the landfills anyway."

"I know, I know. I hear that every day from *Daed*." She lifted Patty and kissed her on her pudgy cheek before adjusting the crocheted blanket to make it tighter.

Martha watched her friend as she walked away. Leaving the Amish wasn't even an option for Martha. First of all, she loved being Amish. Once she took her kneeling vows, she'd be fully committed. At that point, if she left, she'd be excommunicated. Being shunned was the worst thing that could happen to an Amish person, so forget pretty clothes, travel and disposable diapers. Her future was already decided for her. The only question was, who would she spend her life with?

Maybe she hadn't yet met the man of her dreams. Maybe she'd better stop dreaming and head for home. Tomorrow she was headed to Lewistown. A new adventure. She had mixed feelings, but it was only a month, so whatever lay ahead, she could handle it.

Chapter Five

"And these are my little terrors, or treasures, depending on the moment," a very pregnant Deborah said, pointing to her four-year-old triplets. Matthew, Mark, and Luke showed no interest in their new sitter as she attempted to engage them with a cheery greeting. Instead of responding, they chased each other around the long narrow kitchen, tripping over wooden toys and two terrified cats, who narrowly escaped being trampled by six little feet.

"They're cute," Martha managed to say as she looked around the cluttered room. Dishes were stacked in the sink, along with grubby pots and leftover crusts and apple cores. The trash can, which sat in the middle of the room overflowed with paper towels and miscellaneous broken objects, mostly plastic toys. This was going to be a challenge.

"My husband should be home soon. He went fishing with some friends. Haven't seen him since six this morning when I helped with the milking."

"Mercy, how do you do that when you're so close to…to…"

"No choice. Wait till you get married. You'll know what I'm talking about. Amish women do the work of two."

"Oh."

"There's some *kaffi* left from this morning. Do you want me to heat some up for you?"

"No, that's fine." Martha set her small suitcase next to the table and waited to be shown to her room.

"You'll be on the couch in the next room, if you want to put your things in there."

"Sure, that's fine." She lifted the case and followed her hostess into the next room, which was equally messy and had a strong odor of popcorn. It was obvious the youngsters needed to have their clothes changed and after setting her suitcase in the furthest corner of the room, she offered to help with the boys.

"That would be nice of you. I just haven't had time. I need to get a load of clothes washed."

"It's kind of late in the day to hang them out," Martha said as she noted the time on her watch. It was nearly three in the afternoon.

"Oh, I hang them in the basement most days. Sometimes it's eight at night before I get around to the wash. These *kinner* keep me pretty busy, plus feeding the stock and tending to the garden. I don't know how I'll manage when the next two arrive."

"You're due when?" Martha asked before rounding up the first child to change into clean trousers and shirt.

"Yesterday, actually, but it may be a couple days yet."

"No sign?"

"A few pains is all. I have my *boppli* in the hospital. Last time they came two weeks early and the midwife wanted me in the hospital in case they needed help."

"*Gut* idea."

"They weighed over five pounds each. You think I'm big now!" Deborah grinned over and grabbed Luke, who was racing past her at that moment. "You're getting your dirty clothes changed, little one. Now behave for Cousin Martha."

She handed the squirming child over to Martha and pointed to the narrow staircase. "First room on the right. There's a basket of clean clothes there. He can do it himself, but sometimes it's easier to help. Takes less time. No room for a dresser with the three small beds in there. I sure appreciate you helping me out. I should have asked you to come out a month ago."

Martha held tightly to the little boy's hand as they made their way up the stairs to the assigned room. That, too, was a disaster. Soiled clothes sat in piles on the floor and two wicker baskets with clean, but unfolded clothes were shoved under one of the beds. Where were the poor girl's family members? Why wasn't she given some help before now? Already, Martha began to think ahead to her trip back home where her orderly, exceptionally clean home suddenly beckoned. How on earth did Deborah stand living this way? And now two more *kinner* were on the way. A total nightmare!

As she helped the boy with his fresh socks, Deborah appeared holding the other two by their hands. "You may want to tag them somehow so you don't get confused. If you ask them their names, they usually pretend they're one of the others. When my *mamm* helps out, she ties a piece of different color yarn to their wrists. Want me to find some?"

"That might be a *gut* idea. They sure do look alike."

"Don't tie that stuff on us. We'll tell her the truth, *Mamm*. Honest," Mark said.

"Well, okay, but if you start playing games with Cousin Martha, we'll have to use the yarn." She turned to Martha. "Even Ebenezer has trouble sometimes. Of course, he never even changed them and wouldn't know how to dress them even now."

"Of course," Martha said nodding, though in her mind she questioned the arrangement. If it's one at a time, maybe she could agree, but who on earth could handle three at once? Without help!

Supper was thin chicken broth with leftover corn added. There was store-purchased white bread, too. The boys never sat, but leaned against their mother occasionally so she could spoon in a mouthful of the lukewarm soup from time to time. Heaven knew if they each got their share or if one child kept returning, leaving the others to make do with a few bites of bread.

Ebenezer was a man of few words and once he was introduced, he pretty much avoided Martha. In fact, he pretty much avoided everyone in the family. He had returned home with three small brook trout, which would be the main meal the next day. He had managed to clean them first, which surprised Martha. She figured he'd add that to his wife's list.

After the meal, there was no attempt to have devotions as was the norm in most Amish households, but she did notice that he sat for a while with a Bible in his lap. When she looked closer, his eyes were closed. Perhaps he was praying. A few moments later, she heard a rumble from his chair as he snored rhythmically until one of the boys accidentally bumped the side of his chair, at which point, he rose and went up to bed without uttering a word.

Martha helped Deborah prepare the boys for bed. They were given warm milk to calm them down and after about an hour of fussing and tossing stuffed animals and pillows over the sides of the beds, it quieted down.

Deborah sat for about twenty minutes in the sitting room across from Martha. "I hope you'll be comfortable on the couch. I'll get you a pillow and a quilt. Don't worry about the boys. You may hear them awake during the night, but I'll take care of them. You'll need your sleep."

"Mercy, you sure don't get much rest. I don't know how you do it."

"When *Mamm*'s back isn't bothering her, she helps me sometimes, but she watches my *bruder*'s *kinner* when his wife feels poorly. She's in a family way again and she's not strong like me. Now my one *schwester*, Hazel, comes by a lot, so we manage."

"I'll help you as much as possible, Deborah, but I have to admit, it's a bit overwhelming."

Deborah nodded. "*Jah*, it is. I hope we can slow down adding to the family for a little while after the twins are born."

"It would be a pretty *gut* idea, if you ask me."

"Ebenezer wants a big family."

"I guess so, but you're the one doing all the work."

"Oh, he provides us with venison and fish and rabbit. We never go hungry. Not too hungry anyway. And my *mamm* and *daed* bring us produce from their garden. Mine is pretty sparse. I have more weeds than vegetables, I'm afraid."

"I'll try to do some weeding for you tomorrow."

"I sure do appreciate you being here." Deborah's eyes began to fill up. She stood up and headed for the stairs. "I'll get your quilt and all." Martha followed her up to save her a trip.

"See you in the morning," Martha whispered as she turned to go back down the stairs. She had the quilt and pillow in one arm and held a kerosene lamp in the other.

Not to Martha's surprise, the sofa was quite uncomfortable, but after removing a few blocks from under the cushion and plumping up the pillow, she was able to fall asleep. Twenty-nine days left. It seemed like a very long time.

Chapter Six

Martha was awakened by a noisy commotion coming from the upstairs as the triplets ran up and down the hallway above her head. Reprimands from their mother added to the noise volume as she tried to herd them together.

Ebenezer closed the kitchen door behind him as he left for the barn, without attempting to soften the thud which resounded into the sitting room. It was still dark out, but Martha was used to rising early and she quickly dressed in a worn work dress and then used the small lavatory off the kitchen.

She went up to help with the triplets and between her and Deborah, they were soon washed and changed into the fresh clothing they'd put on the afternoon before. They were ready to begin their day. Luke insisted on going down the stairs on his own. He turned and slid down the railing. The other two thumped noisily down the steps. There was just enough light from the kerosene lamp at the foot of the stairs to keep them from falling. The custom was for Ebenezer to use it on his way down and then leave it on a small table at the foot of the stairs to offer enough light for the others to follow.

Each of the boys had their own chair and Martha was surprised to see they actually sat for their breakfast, which consisted of dry Cheerios and apple juice, which Deborah placed in sippy cups. It appeared that more cereal ended up on the floor than in their tummies, but Deborah took it all in stride and swept up the debris without a word. She left the soiled dishes stacked in the sink as she proceeded to go upstairs to sort through the dirty laundry and prepare a load of clothes to wash.

While she was gone, Martha filled the sink with soapy water and began washing the dishes from breakfast, along with pots she found on the stove from the day before. The stove needed a scrubbing and eventually she found some sponges with abrasive backing and a half-filled cleanser can, which she used to clean. Once the dishes were done, she sprinkled cleanser into the sink and let it do its job. Everything she touched was sticky and needed a good solid cleaning. As she worked her way along the counters she heard Deborah return with a basket full of soiled laundry.

"How do you feel today?" Martha asked her as she rinsed the cleanser off the porcelain sink.

"A little crampy. Nothing too bad. How did you sleep?"

"Fine. I think I could have slept on nails last night."

"*Jah*, I know the feeling. Sometimes I don't even remember hitting the bed. Since you're here helping, I'm going down to the cellar to start a load. Do you mind keeping an eye on the boys? Usually, I have to drag them down with me, but it's hard to get anything done with them pulling everything out of the basket to use as costumes or chasing each other around."

"*Nee*, that's fine. You take your time. I'm done here and I'll go watch them in the sitting room. Any restrictions?"

"*Jah*, don't let them stand on the coffee table—or punch each other. Wrestling is okay as long as you don't see blood." She grinned over as she made her way over to the door to the basement.

The boys were in rare form and paid no attention to Martha's requests to slow down or be more gentle with each other. Their playtime bordered on wartime and she watched in horror as they tackled each other and grabbed each other's hair, yanking with all their might. This was met with screams and retaliation. Goodness! If this was what was ahead of her, she just might choose the single life. She'd never been around such unruly children in all her life!

Deborah appeared and didn't seem to notice her children were demolishing the room. The cushions had been pulled off the sofa, and the quilt Martha used, turned into a roof as it laid over an upside-down chair. The boys took turns hiding under it, as the others pranced around before yanking it off the chair to expose the one underneath.

"How about some tea?" Deborah asked Martha. She seemed oblivious to the chaos.

"Uh, sure. Is it safe to leave them here alone?"

"There's nothing they can get into that they haven't already done. I need to start the sausage for Ebenezer. He'll be in for his breakfast soon."

"Would you like me to start bread for dinner?"

Deborah looked astonished at the suggestion. "Really? That would be great. I hope the yeast will rise. I haven't used it in nearly a year."

"It should be okay. While you're working on breakfast, I'll get the bread rising. Where's the flour?"

She pointed to a closed door at the end of the kitchen. "That's my pantry in there. You'll find everything you need. Even the bowls. They're on the top shelf. I'll leave the counter to the right of the sink for you. Ebenezer will be thrilled to get homemade bread. The only time we have any is when my *schwesters* bring some. I expect Hazel will be by later to lend a hand. She usually comes every day for a while. My *mudder* needs her to do most of the cleaning, now that her back is hurting, so I can't always count on her showing up."

"Oh, I'm so glad you get help."

"Lots of people stop by to help, thank the Lord, but when I'm in the hospital, I'll need someone here full time. Ebenezer hasn't a clue to running a house."

You're not too far behind, Martha thought and immediately upbraided herself for having such an unkind thought. "I guess most men don't," she added quickly.

As she kneaded the large mound of yeasty dough, she thought back to her home. She had loved watching her mother make bread when she was a child and had figured her mother had magic hands to take such common items and end up with the rich crusty bread, which attended each meal in their home. Most of the time it was white bread, but on occasion, her mother added wheat or rye flour for taste. And sometimes, she allowed Martha to help her with the cinnamon buns. Martha loved sprinkling the sugar and cinnamon and adding plump raisins to the flattened dough. She would sit patiently while the yummy bread baked in the oven and then her mother would butter both ends for her, adding thin white icing to the tops. Nothing would ever taste that good again.

Maybe she'd bake some for the boys while Deborah was in the hospital. Dare she attempt something with those little hoodlums though?

Ebenezer came in, ate, and left, barely saying a word.

When Deborah went outside to hang the first load of clothes, she took the boys with her, giving Martha the perfect opportunity to scrub down the kitchen floor. The red and white linoleum tiles were so sticky, she removed her shoes so they too wouldn't get grease on them. Her feet would be easier to wash. She folded an already soiled terry towel to cushion her knees and worked with a scrub brush she'd found in a utility closet. With vinegar and detergent and hot water, she was able to lift most of the dirt easily. The hardest part was moving all the furniture and toys away first to allow for a thorough cleaning.

When Deborah returned, Martha had completed her job and was carrying the bucket of water to the door to dump outside.

Deborah's mouth dropped open. "Wow! It looks *wunderbaar*! *Danki*! You are so kind."

Martha noticed tears forming in the girl's eyes.

"I'm happy to do it for you. This afternoon, I'll try to get the bathroom done."

"I never expected you to clean for me, too. I just hoped for help with the *buwe*."

"Well I'm trying to get things done now, while you're still here. When you go in to the hospital, I'll be busy just following the *kinner* around, I'm afraid."

"Oh, *jah*, so true. I think my time is coming real

soon. I had a showing this morning and my cramps are getting stronger."

"Deb, I think we should tell Ebenezer. He'll want to get you to the hospital. Is there a phone nearby we can use to call your doctor?"

"*Jah*, just down the road about a quarter mile. You're probably right. They may come real quick-like this time. Would you go tell him?"

"Sure. Is he in the barn?"

"I think he's out in the field checking the corn. He'll hear you if you yell loud enough."

Martha went out to find him. The boys were in a fenced-in area throwing sand at each other. They didn't even look her way as she passed by. Fortunately, Ebenezer was hoeing between the front rows. When he looked up, she noted he had nice blue eyes—even kind looking. She told him about his wife and he nodded. "I'll be right there. I'll call for a ride. The buggy might be too slow and bumpy for her right now."

He took off for the community phone as Martha returned to the house. She felt perspiration under her arms. She was nervous. It was quite a responsibility to watch someone else's children when she barely knew them. She sent up a prayer to ask for strength and wisdom in handling the boys and of course for their safety as well as a quick—though not *too* quick—delivery of the twins.

An hour later, she found herself alone with the children. She checked the rising bread, then patted it down for a second rise. The boys had quieted down somewhat after their parents left them. Matthew sat on the floor, his arms surrounding his legs. He wasn't even playing and was the only one who seemed concerned to have his mother leave. The other two were tussling with one of the cat's stuffed mice and it split open, scattering catnip all over the clean floor. Martha reached for a dust pan and cleaned it up. There wasn't much point in trying to discipline the boys with so little time. It was a matter of keeping them safe, clean and fed—not her responsibility to correct every little thing.

There was a knock on the back door and she looked up to see the smiling face of Hazel, Deborah's younger sister. Good. Company. She opened the door and introduced herself. The boys, who had raced into the sitting room after one of their cats, heard a new voice and all three came running into the kitchen to see who had arrived. Hazel grabbed them one at a time and gave them effusive hugs and greetings. They received her attention with glee and miraculously settled down. Martha hoped to learn her secret.

Chapter Seven

Hazel was great company for Martha, and the two of them worked non-stop cleaning the house as the boys settled down and built towers with their large Legos on the sparkling kitchen floor. The weather was perfect for drying clothes so Martha stripped the beds and gathered towels and clothing from the floors of the rooms. Hazel sang as she worked and set up the ironing board to tackle an enormous pile of men's shirts, two of Deborah's church dresses and three cotton tablecloths, which had been sitting in their crinkled state for almost a year.

Around five in the afternoon, Ebenezer showed up, grinning widely. The twins were identical girls and they were already named Mary and Miriam. They each weighed in at six pounds and would be coming home the very next day.

Ebenezer stopped long enough to have a plate of sliced ham with homemade potato salad and then he went out to milk the cows and take care of the other livestock.

Hazel left shortly after that, but before she left, she helped Martha clean up from supper and change the

boys into night clothes. Martha was ever so grateful for
her help and gave Hazel a hug before she took off. She
promised to return the next day, hopefully to be there
in time to greet the new arrivals.

By the time Martha was done, it was eight o'clock.
Ebenezer went to bed as soon as he finished reading his
Bible and nodded to Martha as he climbed the stairs.
"*Gut nacht*," he said, smiling. She hadn't seen a smile
that broad on the man's face before, and she was pleased
that he seemed happy about his new family members.

Martha checked on the boys, who had fallen asleep
without a fuss, and then took time to brush her teeth and
wash up before changing into night clothes and wrapping
herself in the homemade quilt, which smelled wonderful-
gut from being laundered and dried in the outdoors. It
had been a good day in every way. She hadn't thought
even once about Daniel Beiler, so life did go on. She fell
asleep half way through her prayers.

Ebenezer left the next morning for the hospital, using
his English driver once again. He had risen even earlier
than usual in order to take care of all his chores before
leaving. As Martha encouraged the boys to sit at their
places, she poured hot oatmeal into plastic bowls and set
them in front of the children. After a few fusses, they
concentrated on their meal. A knock came at the door
and Martha looked through the door window to see an
attractive young Amishman in his mid-twenties grinning and waving.

When she opened the door, he introduced himself as
Eb's cousin and Hazel's neighbor. He relayed her message that she'd be unable to arrive at the house until close
to noon. "I'm on my way to work, so I told her I'd give
you the message."

He stood at the door, twisting the rim of his straw hat in his hands, his baby blue eyes staring directly into Martha's. Her heart flipped more than once. Should she invite him in? After all, she really didn't know the man, but surely he was okay since Hazel wouldn't have sent him over if he was dangerous in any way.

"*Danki*. We're doing fine. Uh…would you care for a cup of *kaffi*?" she asked as she wiped her hands on her apron.

"Don't mind if I do. I don't have to be at work for another half hour and it's only up the road five minutes."

She waved him over to the table. The boys stopped spooning in their cereal and grinned over at him.

"*Hallo, buwe*. Are you excited to have two *schwesters*?"

"I don't know if they fully understand," Martha said as she filled a mug with coffee and placed it on the mat in front of him.

"I guess you're right. I know they're pretty young."

Then Luke surprised them by answering. "*Jah, Daed* said. We got us two *boppli* and *Mamm*'s better now."

"Well she wasn't really sick," Martha began and then stopped. She turned to the man, who at this point was still nameless. "I'm sorry, I didn't catch your name."

"I guess because I didn't give it." He chuckled and then nodded. "It's Paul Yoder and you're Martha Troyer. Right?"

"*Jah*, you got that right."

"It's real nice of you to come and help out. I know Deborah and Eb could use the extra help. It's gonna be a bit wild for a while with all these *kinner*."

"I'm only staying for a month," she said as she handed over the sugar bowl.

"I take it plain, but thanks anyway."

The boys returned to their cereal and then one at a time, pushed away from the table to get back to the important things in life, like building towers and pushing toy trucks around on the floor.

Martha asked Paul about his job and discovered he worked as a carpenter for a small Amish shop that made furniture. It was obvious that he enjoyed his work. His eyes lit up as he discussed his latest project. They had just installed cherry wood cabinets in a new kitchen. "It had six bedrooms and four baths. The family had only two *kinner*, but they sure liked a lot of space. The house was nearly 4000 square feet. That's big!"

"I guess so," she said. "Were they Amish?"

"*Nee*, English. He's a doctor and she teaches school. Nice people."

"I don't know many English people," she said, stirring cream into her coffee. "Just the driver we use. He's very nice."

"Most of the ones I've met are *gut* people. Not that different from us in some ways."

"Oh, but they sure dress different."

"*Jah*, that's for sure and for certain. I like the way our women dress better. Like you. Even though you're wearing an old *frack*, you still look nice."

"Oh, is it that obvious that it's old?"

"I didn't mean to offend you," he said, as color rose in his neck. "I know you're here to work. And it's clean. That's what matters."

"And I did bring a church dress for Sunday, though I don't know if we'll make it this week, since it's already Friday. It will depend on Deborah and the new *boppli*."

"I bet she'll make it. She came to church three days

after the triplets arrived. That woman is as strong as my driving horse. *Gut* Amish stock."

"I don't know if I'd be that strong."

"So are you spoken for yet?" he asked, tilting his head slightly.

"*Nee*. Not yet. Maybe never at the rate things are going."

"Not possible. You probably have a ton of guys interested."

"You're flattering me. I'm not sure I like it."

"Sorry again. I'm just a truth teller." He cleared his throat. "So you'll be here all month?"

"That's the plan."

"Maybe you'll let me show you around the area sometime, if you're not too busy."

"I probably will be, but it was nice of you to ask."

"Well, if you ever do find you have time on your hands, you can let me know. I stop by often. Eb and I are cousins and we went to school together, so we stay in close touch. He's my fishing partner sometimes when I don't have to work."

"*Jah*, tonight we're having trout he caught. Fish is *gut* for you."

"It is. Do you ever go fishing?"

"*Nee*. I have no interest, but I like to paint pictures sometimes when I'm not too busy."

"Really? You're an artist?"

Martha laughed aloud. "You can't call me an artist. I just like to paint flowers. I love to do roses. They're my very favorite flower. I planted three new bushes this spring."

"What color are they?"

"They're peachy. Just so beautiful. I wish I had a camera sometimes."

"*Jah*, I have a friend who's a Mennonite and he takes pictures for me sometimes, but I keep them in a drawer so I won't get into trouble. That's one thing I kinda disagree on. Like, what's the harm?"

"I know. I feel the same, but we have to accept the *Ordnung*."

"*Jah*, and I do. I'm getting baptized this year."

"I need to get baptized, too. I'd never want to leave the Plain life."

"Neither would I. Well, I'd better run along now. I don't want to be late." He stood and then carried his mug to the sink before heading for the door. "Nice to meet you Martha Troyer and maybe I'll stop by tomorrow to meet the new *maedel*."

"That would be nice. I can't wait to see them. I bet they're adorable."

"All little *kinner* are cute, but especially little girls."

She smiled over and nodded. "See you then. Have a *gut* day, Paul."

After he left, she stood watching as he climbed into his buggy and clucked at his horse. After he left, she checked the small mirror in the bathroom. She sure looked disheveled. Who would have expected a man to just drop in like that—and such an attractive one to boot. Tomorrow, she'd be ready. Her green dress, though old, was in a lot better condition than this one and the hardest jobs had been accomplished, so she wouldn't need to wear such a raggedy outfit.

Chapter Eight

Martha scurried about, redding up the house for the returning *mamm* and her new twin girls. She made spaghetti sauce, using homemade sausage for flavor. After starting bread dough, she changed the boys into fresh shirts after bathing them quickly in the large enamel tub. Since the hot water didn't last long, she kept the water level low, much to their distress since they loved playing in the water, sailing plastic toy boats around and torpedoing each other's toys.

Once they were presentable, she sat them down at the kitchen table and gave them puzzles to put together while she washed and dried the dishes from earlier. She hadn't seen much of Ebenezer as the driver had picked him up around nine and before that he was in the barn. She noticed he cleaned himself well before leaving, changing into a fresh shirt and pair of trousers. Even his vest looked spotless. When he tried, he presented a pleasant picture of a good looking Amishman in his prime.

While preparing a large pot of corn chowder, she heard a rap on the back door. Expecting Hazel, she called out to enter. After the door opened, she caught sight of the sky-blue-eyed Paul, grinning widely, exposing his perfectly even ivory teeth.

He held a paper bag in his one hand. "Here, this is for our *kaffi* break. My *mamm* made crumb cake this morning and it's still warm. Hope you like it."

"*Danki.* How nice of you. Let me calm the *buwe* down first. I told them they could play with their Legos if they promised to stop hitting each other."

"They're a wild bunch, I'm afraid. I bet you were tired last night."

"Oh, *jah*. That's the truth. I don't know how Deborah will manage when I leave. Five little ones. Mercy."

"Hazel will have to help out."

"She's such a nice person. She'll make a *gut* Amish wife someday."

Paul looked down at the floor and then coughed into his hand. Martha suspected a relationship between the two young people and wondered if they were a couple.

"She's a pretty *maed*, too," she offered.

"*Jah*, she is."

"Does she have a fella?"

"You'd have to ask her, I'm afraid. We don't talk that much anymore."

"Oh. But once you did?"

"Okay. *Jah*. We were interested in each other once, but no longer."

"Oh, I'm sorry."

"Actually, I'm the one who broke it off."

"It's not my business. Forgive me if I'm bringing up old wounds."

"*Nee*, it's okay. Really. I just didn't love her. Like? *Jah*. Very much, but I have to feel much more to commit to marriage. I'm still young yet. I'll find the right girl someday, I'm certain of that."

"Same age as Ebenezer, right?" she asked.

"*Jah*, twenty-five."

"He's gonna be way ahead of you," she said with a giggle. "Five *kinner* already."

Paul's face flushed as he diverted his eyes to the bag he'd brought.

"Oh, let me start a fresh pot of *kaffi*," Martha said quickly. "I only have enough for one small cup left."

"What time will they be coming home with the twins?" he asked as he removed the crumb cake and placed it on a plate, which she had set on the table.

"I'm not sure. Probably soon. Aren't you working today?"

"Actually, I have the day off. My boss is closing the shop for a couple days, so I figured I could be of help to Eb. I'll hang around, if that's okay with you, and then I'll milk the cows later. I imagine there are other chores I can do. I can even wash dishes, if that would help you out."

"That's so nice of you, but I'm okay. So far."

With that, Luke came charging into the kitchen, his face crimson. "Mark is bad. He hit me right here," he said pointing to his cheek.

"Excuse me, Paul, I think I'm needed." She went swiftly into the front room and sat Mark on a small wooden chair, faced away from his brothers. Then she crouched down and faced him. "Now Mark, you know better than to hit someone."

"He hit first," he replied, turning his head to glare at his brother.

"Nope," Matthew said loudly. "I saw everything. Mark started it. He's a bad *bu*."

"Then you'll have to sit here in the corner by yourself for fifteen minutes as punishment."

"That's like forever," he said, tearing up.

"Not forever. That's way longer," Matthew said as he folded his arms.

"I'll set the timer and call you when your time is up. Okay?"

"I guess." Mark scowled as he sat facing the plain white wall.

Martha returned to find Paul leafing through the Budget Newspaper, which had arrived that morning.

"Any chance you can stay beyond the month?" he asked as she took a seat across from him and cut off a piece of crumb cake, moving it to a butter plate.

"I doubt it. My *mudder* has problems and I feel guilty being away from her this long."

"I'm sorry to hear that."

"I'm an only child, so it puts a lot of responsibility on me as my parents age."

"I imagine so. Is your *daed* in *gut* health?"

"*Jah*, he's very strong. He's fifty-five, which isn't that old, I guess."

"My parents are in their sixties, but they're in great shape. I have three older brothers and two older sisters."

"That would be so wonderful. I always wanted to be part of a large family, but my *mudder* couldn't have any more after me. Someday I want to give them lots of grandchildren to love."

He smiled over and nodded. "You're very sweet, you know."

She blushed and took another bite of cake. "Your *mamm* is a *gut* baker. This is yummy."

"*Jah*, she loves to bake. Lucky I don't weigh three hundred pounds."

"You are a nice size. For a man. I mean…"

He laughed and drank from his mug. "*Danki*, I think."

If she had said that to Daniel, he would have been annoyed at the way it came out. Paul seemed to find her comments amusing, which pleased her. He laughed a lot and smiled even more. Another nice quality.

They discussed the weather, the crops, their communities—everything. He seemed genuinely interested in everything she had to say.

When the buzzer went off, she went in and told Mark he could play now, but first he needed to apologize to his brother. It almost sounded sincere and Mark nodded and then grinned. "I was kinda mean, too. Let's build a red wall."

When she turned back to go into the kitchen, she saw Paul had been standing and watching the exchange. He nodded at the boys and offered to help them with the wall, if they got stuck.

"You seem to enjoy *kinner*," she said as they headed back to the kitchen.

"Oh, *jah*, I hope to have at least seven or eight *kinner* someday."

"Me, too." They sat and resumed their conversation until they were interrupted by the sound of car tires on the gravel driveway. "I bet that's Deborah and Ebenezer with the twins," she said, jumping up from the chair and heading out the door. Paul was right behind her.

Eb opened the back door of the auto and reached for his wife's hand, helping her to the steps. Martha greeted her with a gentle hug and guided her up the stairs. Then Eb removed the first car-bed and handed it to Paul, who went swiftly into the kitchen and placed it on a long bench next to the table. Then Eb took out the second one and carried it up the four steps to the kitchen door. After setting the bed down on the kitchen floor, he returned to pay the driver.

"Oh, how adorable!" Martha said as she moved the top of the receiving blanket from the bed resting on the floor, exposing Miriam's ruddy complexion. She was nearly bald, but her head was nicely formed and her lips were like sweet buds, actively sucking the air. Her eyes remained shut.

Paul leaned over and spoke gently to the sleeping baby. "Aren't you a cutey?" he said.

Deborah grinned and nodded in agreement. "They look just the same. I can't tell them apart yet. It's even harder than with the *buwe*. Come see little Mary," she added as she arranged the skewed knitted bonnet away from her eyes. "I gave them different color bonnets."

"Oh my, they do look exactly alike. They are so beautiful," Martha said, tears forming in her eyes. "*Gott*'s miracle."

They all agreed and then they moved the babies into the living room, where the boys were playing rather quietly for a change. When they saw their new sisters and their mother, they ran over and gave a raucous welcome to their new siblings. Eb came in and hushed them down. Then he told them to sit on the sofa and he'd let them take turns holding the babies. The boys obeyed immediately and for a few moments sat hushed as their parents moved the babes from lap to lap. Luke couldn't stop giggling and woke Miriam once, who opened her eyes briefly before resuming sleep.

"How do you feel?" Martha asked Deborah.

"*Gut*, but tired. I may lie down in a while after they nurse again."

Eb removed his daughters from his son's laps and placed Mary in Deborah's arms and handed Miriam to Martha. She held her gently, cooing softly at the sleeping babe. "She's so lovely. I can't wait to have a *boppli* of my own."

"Better find a *gut* man first," Eb teased. "Like Paul here. He's looking, right, Paul?"

Paul's neck became beet-red and Martha quickly switched the subject to the hospital care. "Did you have nice nurses?" she asked her friend.

"They were wonderful-*gut*. Stayed with me the whole time. We stopped at my parents' home on the way back from the hospital. We only stayed a few minutes. My *schwesters* couldn't wait to see their new nieces. *Mamm* will be by in a while with Wanda, and Hazel will be here soon, after she does a few chores."

"Maybe I should leave then," Paul said, looking over at Deborah.

"Don't be silly. She's not upset with you. She realized it wouldn't work out between you two. You're way too different."

"I never meant to hurt her."

Deborah shook her head. "You're a kind man. No one ever thought it was intentional." She glanced over at Martha, who pretended to be unaware of their discussion. "Maybe *Gott* has brought the right one for you, Paul."

Oh my. Martha wished she was anywhere but there.

"Don't embarrass Martha," Eb said with a grin. "She's probably promised to a *gut* Amishman back in her hometown."

"Uh, I think we need to change the subject," Paul said, glancing down at his feet. "Martha and I barely know each other and you're embarrassing both of us."

Upon finishing his statement, a buggy was heard approaching the front entrance. Eb was the closest to the front door and went to open it for Hazel, who pulled over and tethered the horse to the front post. "I hope the *maedel* aren't still sleeping. I can't wait to see the color of their eyes."

"They are still asleep, but come in and we'll get someone to make a fresh pot of *kaffi*," Eb said.

When Hazel stepped in, she looked over at Paul, who still had a blush in his cheeks. "*Hallo*, Paul. What do you think of the *boppli*? Aren't they adorable?"

"*Jah*, they are very cute." He went towards the hallway to the kitchen. "I think I'll check your goats, Eb. They weren't eating much earlier."

"I'll come out after we get the *boppli* settled in."

"Take your time. I'm here to help you."

Hazel turned toward Martha. "Paul is a *gut* friend, Martha. You'll see how helpful he can be."

"*Jah*, I believe it. And his *mamm* is a *gut* baker. He brought crumb cake and there is still some to go around."

"I love crumb cake," Hazel said, nodding. "I'll make the *kaffi*, if you want," she said to Deborah.

"*Jah*, that would be nice. I'm going to go upstairs and feed the twins. Eb, you can give me a hand while I carry Mary. I need the car beds upstairs."

"Sure."

"Let me carry Miriam upstairs for you," Martha said,

anxious to leave the room. Though the conversation sounded normal enough, she could feel the tension and it wasn't pleasant. Did Paul and Hazel still have feelings for each other. For some reason, she hoped not. Surely, she didn't have eyes for Paul. Was she rebounding now that Daniel Beiler appeared to be disinterested? Goodness, she and Paul lived too far apart to have a meaningful relationship.

She carried the baby in her arms, inhaling the lovely baby smell as she kissed the child's bare scalp. So dear.

Chapter Nine

The men were out in the barn, and the boys were supposed to be napping, though giggles and scuffles were ever present. With Deborah nursing her babies upstairs, Martha and Hazel cleaned up the kitchen from the snack and then Martha placed the risen dough in the oven while Hazel swept the floor. "Those *buwe* sure can make a mess," she said as she retrieved partial cookies and crumbs from the toast they'd eaten earlier.

"They've been better than I thought they'd be," Martha said as she stirred the pasta sauce. "I guess I should put water on for the spaghetti. I bet everyone's hungry."

"Don't set a place for me, I'm not staying," Hazel said as she dumped the debris from the dustpan into the trash.

"Oh, we made plenty of food, Hazel. Please stay."

Hazel set the broom and pan aside and crossed her arms. "It's too hard on me—seeing Paul. I haven't gotten over him, I guess."

"I'm sorry. Were you seeing him for a long time?"

"Only about six months, but I thought we had something special. He nearly broke my heart."

"I'm in the middle of a tough time, too," Martha offered. "I thought I had found the man of my dreams, but not so."

"It's so hard, isn't it?" Hazel's eyes misted over. "He was over nearly every other evening to see me and then, boom. Just like that, he said he really didn't love me. I don't know why it took him so long to realize it."

"I'm surprised. You're so sweet and kind."

"He even told me that, but I guess it wasn't enough. Maybe he'll fall for you, Martha."

"Oh, I wouldn't even consider it—especially knowing you still care about him."

"I wouldn't stand in your way. *Gott* may have plans. Who am I to go against His will?"

"Well, first of all, we live too far apart, it would be very hard to get serious with someone you rarely saw. Secondly, I have no interest in him or anyone else. I have to get over Daniel first."

"Did he break up with you, or the other way around?" Hazel asked.

"I don't know if we even broke off. It just seemed to cool off all of a sudden and neither of us has tried to keep it going. Now that I'm here, if he cared at all, he'd write, don't you think?"

"Maybe he's waiting to hear from you. Or don't you care enough to try?"

"I'm not sure what I feel. He's kinda boring, to tell you the truth. Very serious. Rarely smiles."

"Ugh. And you're so happy and smiley. No wonder it didn't work out."

The back door opened and Paul and Eb walked in with Deborah and Hazel's father, Jim, in tow. He was introduced to Martha. After nodding and grunting some kind of greeting, he settled down on a kitchen chair, pulled on his suspenders, and looked over at his son-in-law. "When's my *dochder* bringing the *boppli* down? I barely saw them two with all the women crowding round."

Eb shrugged. "She should be down anytime. Want something to eat?"

"I'll wait for Priscilla. She and Wanda stopped to check the tomatoes. They don't look too healthy if you ask me."

"Haven't had much time to work on 'em."

"You never do. Only find time to hunt and fish. Guess that'll end now with two more *kinner* to take care of. Deborah's gonna need your help."

"She's a strong woman. I think she can handle it."

Paul cleared his throat and Eb and his father-in-law, Jim, stopped talking and looked over at him. "Uh, I'm leaving for home now, but I'll try to stop by tomorrow in case you need help, Eb."

"You don't have to leave, Paul. I'm on my way home," Hazel said.

"Why are you leaving, Hazel?" her father asked. "We're here to have dinner. There ain't anything much to eat back home."

"Well…"

"It's okay, really," Paul emphasized. "I have plans for tonight." He opened the back door and turned briefly to say good-bye to everyone.

Once out of the house, Hazel let out a long sigh. "I hate feeling this way."

"What way?" her father asked.

"Oh, you wouldn't understand."

His frown forced her to soften her tone. "I like Paul Yoder, more than I should, *Daed*. That's all."

"Well, marry the lad."

"He hasn't asked me."

"Shame on him."

Eb held back a grin. "It don't work that way."

"Well, it did in my time. Think Priscilla and I were crazy in love when we married? No sir, but she was a fine Amish lady of *gut* character and she knew I was hard working and would be faithful. That's what counts."

"Some of us look for more," Eb said. "The only *maed* I ever even liked was Deborah. It's gotten us through rough times."

"Rough? You have it easy. Five *kinner* already. Some women never have any."

Martha disliked Deborah's father from the moment she saw him. He was not only gruff, but unkempt as well. What an upbringing for his children. Yet, Hazel was a sweetheart. She must take after her mother. With that, Priscilla came into the kitchen, carrying a handful of small tomatoes. "This is all I could find that were ripe, but better than nothing, I guess."

Her words did not encourage positive feelings about her personality to Martha. When Deborah's mother saw Martha standing next to the sink, she stopped and nodded. "You're the girl what's been helping our Deborah."

"*Jah*, congratulations on your new *grossdochders*. They're real cute."

"They look like most *boppli*. Don't get cute till their older." She laid the tomatoes on the side of the sink and wiped her hands on her apron.

"Oh, I think they're adorable," Martha said, her voice rising slightly.

"Deborah's gonna have her hands full now. Hope she don't expect me to show up every day to wash diapers."

"I'll be here every day, especially when Martha has to leave," Hazel said, glaring over at her mother, who totally ignored it.

Goodness, Hazel and Deborah must have been switched in the hospital! They were so different from their parents.

"Guess Deborah is upstairs," Priscilla added as she made her way to the staircase at the end of the hall. "Call when dinner's ready."

Martha and Hazel exchanged glances and began preparing a salad together while Eb and her father argued about the state of their crops.

"Sorry," Hazel whispered.

"Don't apologize. It's fine."

"*Nee*, it's not. Sometimes I want to scream. All I ever hear is complaining and bickering. At this point, I'd marry the first man who asked me."

The men's voices increased in volume and then they went out the door together, slamming the screen door behind them, still arguing over the size of their prospective corn crops.

Hazel let out a long sigh. "I envy you. You'll be going home in a couple weeks."

"You could pay us a visit, you know."

"Not while Deborah needs me. I thought my *schwester*, Wanda, was coming, too. You haven't met her yet."

With that, another member of the Miller family, came into the kitchen from outside. She had a handful of fresh parsley and laid it next to the tomatoes by the sink. She managed a smile and nodded towards Martha. "You're Martha, right?"

"*Jah*, and you must be Wanda. Congratulations."

"On what? Oh, the *boppli*. Sure. They're pretty little *boppli*, aren't they?"

Martha nodded. "Oh, they're beautiful. And big for twins, too."

"*Jah*, my *schwester* knows how to produce *boppli*, that's for sure."

"And for certain," Hazel added with a grin.

"Need help?" Wanda asked.

"*Nee*, we have everything under control. We're just making salad. You can go up to be with Deborah, if you want," Hazel added.

"How was *Mamm* when she came in? Man, she was on a rampage earlier about *Daed* tracking dirt on her clean floor."

"That's a definite no-no," Hazel said in an aside to Martha.

"*Jah*, no one likes having mud on a clean floor," Martha said.

"It was barely a dot, but that's the way it goes at our house," Wanda added, with a look in Hazel's direction.

Hazel nodded and turned to Martha. "Wanda is engaged. She's going to be married in November. It hasn't been published yet, but everyone knows."

"I can't wait," Wanda said and Martha figured her enthusiasm was justified.

Once the meal was ready to be served, the family was called down. After the blessing, the serving dishes were passed around and a silent meal followed. Only an occasional request for more food ensued. It was a long meal and Martha counted the days until she could leave.

Chapter Ten

Martha's parents, Sarah and Melvin, worked together picking the plump fresh blueberries from their bushes behind the barn. Sarah had enough already for a pie and at least six jars of jam. She might even have extra to take to her sister, Lizzy, who hinted at wanting some every single year. Sarah wondered why her sister didn't just plant a few bushes of her own. She had plenty of space.

"That sun's hot today," Melvin noted, as he pushed his straw hat back and wiped his damp forehead.

"It's hot every day," Sarah said with a grin.

"Guess you're right, but I feel it more, the older I get."

"Let's go and relax then. We have nearly all the ripe ones picked already. I made sweet tea earlier."

"Now you're talking. Here, give me your basket and I'll carry it over to the house."

"Let's sit under the red maple on the side of the house. It's such a beautiful view from there."

"*Jah*. I'll bring over a couple folding chairs and a table while you pour the tea," he added.

"I'll stop by the *dawdi-haus* and see if my folks want to join us."

"Then I'll bring two more chairs. It's much cooler under the maple, that's for sure."

After laying the two baskets of fresh berries in the kitchen, Melvin went out to the barn to retrieve the folding chairs and a small table for their snack.

Sarah stopped at the *dawdi-haus* and asked her parents if they'd like to join them, and her mother said they'd come out later after they finished reading the Bible together.

Carrying a tea-filled pitcher and glasses, along with a plate of molasses cookies on a floral plastic tray, Sarah made her way carefully along the grass to the shade tree where her husband was already seated. He moved the table about until it was steady and then she placed the tray on it and poured him a glass of the cool amber liquid.

He sat back and drained the first glass and reached for the pitcher to add more. "*Gut.*"

"*Jah*, it's refreshing when you're thirsty."

"Your folks coming out?"

"Pretty soon."

"Heard from Martha yet?" he asked.

"Not yet. Probably today."

"Did you write to her?"

"*Jah*, you know I did. Mailed it two days ago. In fact, you put it in the mailbox for me."

"Oh, *jah*. I forgot. Guess she's pretty busy."

"I wonder if the *boppli* were born yet. Wish we could use phones."

"You know the rules on that one."

"It's the one rule I wish our bishop would change."

"He ain't gonna, Sarah. You know that."

"My *daed* might have influence over him."

"Nope."

Sarah passed the plate of cookies and he took three and laid them on a paper napkin.

"He could try," she added.

"Nope. As a deacon, he only helps when people are needy, you know that. Our bishop decides the rules of the *Ordnung*."

"But we're having the rules service soon. You or *Daed* could at least bring it up."

"Big Manny asked about it last year. Don't you remember? It got a little heated."

"I guess so, but I know some districts allow cell phones and I ain't seen the end of the world happen yet."

"Now Sarah, as your husband, I'm telling you not to bring it up. I won't be happy if you do."

"Don't worry about it. Have another cookie. Here comes *Mamm*. Let's let it drop, Mel."

He grunted and then stood to open up the third chair for his mother-in-law.

Sarah realized she had upset her husband, but she just couldn't figure out why it would be a bad thing to have phones. That way she'd be able to talk to her daughter while she was away. She missed her so much. But her husband had made it clear—she was to let the matter rest.

Martha woke up to the wails of the new babies coming from upstairs. It was already six o'clock and she'd slept right through her wind-up alarm clock. Swiftly twisting her long dark brown hair into a bun and placing her *kapp* over her head, she reached for fresh clothing and dressed before knocking on Deborah's bedroom door. Perhaps she could calm one of the babies down to give Deborah a chance to nurse the other.

When she went into the bedroom, she found her friend in tears. "I don't think I have enough milk. They just keep fussing. What can I do?"

"We can use the formula they sent home with you, just until your supply catches up."

"Think that would be okay? I don't want to have problems."

"I'm sure it will be just fine. Want me to go down and make up a bottle?"

"Oh, *jah*. You're such a big help. Eb doesn't do anything for me. And I hear the *buwe* fighting. How can I ever manage when you leave?"

Martha reached for a tissue and handed it over. "By the time I leave, you'll be into a *gut* routine." She sounded more optimistic than she believed in her heart. Poor girl. How exhausting. "I'll take care of the boys as soon as I can. First the bottle. Maybe I should do two and once the boys settle down, I can help you with the twins."

Deborah nodded as she sniffed and wiped her eyes with her sleeve. She lifted Mary from her crib and held her over her shoulder while patting her back, but nothing seemed to help.

As Martha passed the triplets' room, she scolded them for the rumpus and told them to dress themselves and get downstairs. Then she went down and set up places at the table for the boys, poured Cheerios into three separate bowls and placed them at their seats. After reading the directions for the formula, she poured four ounces into each of two bottles and put them into a pan of warm water to take off the chill. The cries of the twins seemed to increase. Soon the boys came tumbling down and made their way to the table, in various stages of dress.

Eb came through the door and took in the scene before him. "Why are the *maedel* screaming?"

"It's a long story, Eb. Right now, please keep an eye on your *sohns* so I can help with the *boppli*."

"I need *kaffi*. Did you make any yet?"

"*Nee*, I did not! You'll have to make a pot yourself!" she said angrily as she grabbed hold of the bottles and stormed upstairs.

When she reached Deborah's bedroom, she felt only slightly calmer. She handed Deborah one of the bottles for Mary and then picked up Mariam and sat on the edge of the bed to feed her. Once they had quieted down and were sucking vigorously at their bottles, Deborah looked over at Martha. "I heard Eb's voice."

"*Jah*."

"Is he watching the *buwe*?"

"I hope so."

"They're quieter now."

"Umm."

"Martha, is everything all right?"

"Sorry. Sure, everything's fine."

"I'm glad Eb came in to help."

"He came in for *kaffi*."

"Oh." Deborah's eyes filled again and Martha regretted adding that last remark, especially in the tone she used. "I'm sure he wanted to help, too," Martha added, more calmly.

"*Nee*. Not Eb. When do you think Hazel will be by?"

"She didn't say, but she'll probably be here soon."

"She's a wonderful-*gut schwester*."

"*Jah*, that she is. You're lucky to have her, Deborah."

"I'm lucky to have you, too. You're so kind."

Guilt filled Martha as she thought how anxious she was to get back home. She was counting the days. But how could she leave this poor young woman with so little help? She should write to her parents and see how they were getting along without her. Perhaps, they'd suggest she stay on another week or so when her time was up. She could probably last that long and surely by then the babies would be easier to care for. Deborah would be stronger, too, and perhaps a miracle would take place and her lazy husband would pitch in and help!

When she went back downstairs after changing the babies and putting them down in their cribs on the other side of Deborah's room, Paul arrived. Eb was still hanging out in the kitchen, coffee yet unmade. He barely said a word to Martha and she knew she'd displeased him. Too bad. He sure displeased her!

Since Paul was there now, she made a full pot of coffee and then prepared a pot of chili for their dinner at noon.

Eb announced he was going out to the barn to fix a piece of equipment. Paul told Eb he'd be out to help after he had his coffee.

"I'll come back for my *kaffi* in ten minutes," Eb said on his way out to the barn. "Hope it will be better than the last pot you made."

Martha felt her blood pressure rise as she gritted her teeth. Paul let out a laugh after the door slammed behind Eb.

"What, pray tell, is funny now?" she said, turning to him with a scowl.

"Oops. Sorry. I just saw how mad that made you."

"Well *jah*! The nerve of that man! You wouldn't believe what a morning we've had here already."

"I'm sorry. I didn't realize. Forgive me for finding it amusing."

She let out a breath. "It's okay. How would you know. Paul, that man is the laziest person I've ever met. I don't know how you can stand being his friend."

"He doesn't know any better. He was catered to all his life."

"Well, I don't know how Deborah is going to handle five *kinner* all by herself."

"Maybe you can stay a little longer. I still haven't shown you around."

"You're kidding, right?" she asked, her brows arching. "I can't get five minutes to myself, and I'm really not complaining, but when Eb makes a comment about the *kaffi*? That goes too far."

"You know what? You *need* a break. When Hazel gets here, I'm taking you for a buggy ride."

"Oh, I couldn't."

"You need a change, Martha. Look how upset you are. It's too much. After all, you're a single girl, you're not used to all these *kinner* around. You said you're an only child, too."

"If, and I mean—*if*, things are calm enough, I'll take you up on your offer. Still not working?"

"Nope. Not until tomorrow and it's a beautiful day out there. I'll take you to some nice gardens nearby. I'll even treat you to lunch."

"Oh, I won't leave before I serve the chili. You can stay and have some with us, if you'd like."

"Why don't you serve them and then we'll leave and

I'll take you to my favorite family restaurant. They do chicken and dumplings just like my *mamm* does."

"Oh, that sounds so nice. I miss my *mamm*'s cooking. I'm afraid I'm not a very *gut* cook."

"Then that's what we'll do."

"Oh, Paul, I don't know…"

"Why?"

"It's just because, I don't want Hazel to be hurt."

"She's over me."

"Maybe not."

"I'm sure she is, Martha. Besides, we're not getting married, we're just going to a diner."

"I guess you're right. Okay, but we don't have to tell her where we're going or anything."

"Whatever you want. Now that *kaffi* looks black enough. I'll go tell Eb. No, better yet, I'll take a mugful out to him and we can have ours by ourselves."

"*Jah*, and three little monsters…sorry, three little *buwe*, too."

"Hey, for once, they're quiet."

"That's when I worry the most. I'll check them while you take Eb's *kaffi* out to him."

Surprisingly, they were busy coloring, bellies down in the sitting room. She tiptoed back to the kitchen and set the pot on the table.

Soon Paul returned and they sat quietly together and chatted. Only an occasional holler reached their ears as Martha and Paul had a relaxing break.

Chapter Eleven

When Hazel arrived, Paul had already gone out to the barn to work with Eb. She had baked brownies and she laid the *toot* on the table before removing her shoes. "How is it going?" she asked Martha, who was wiping down the sink.

"You don't want to know. Eb is worthless."

"He always has been. I warned her about marrying him, but she thought she could change him. Sometimes he can be sweet to her, but most of the time…"

"She's still upstairs with the twins." After filling Hazel in on the rest of the morning, Martha suggested the boys go out and play in the fenced off area where it was equipped with a sandbox, which Paul had added early in the spring.

They ran out, pushing each other and yelling as they went.

"Hush now," Hazel reprimanded. "You'll wake the dead with those voices."

"That's funny," Mark said, not even knowing what "dead" meant.

The twins were sleeping soundly when the women

went upstairs to Deborah's room. She was lying on her bed, still wiping her eyes. "I'm a failure. I don't have enough milk yet. I did better when the *buwe* were born and there were three of them."

Hazel sat on the bed and took her sister's hand. "Goodness, it's way too early to call yourself a failure. It's hard to get adjusted in the beginning. My friend, Milly, had to supplement for the first month and she only had one *boppli*. Give yourself time."

"I think I'm just too exhausted."

Martha took a seat next to Hazel. "Sometimes, *mamms* have to use just formula. It's not the end of the world. *Boppli* still survive if they're not breastfed."

"I guess," Deborah said haltingly. "But it's better for them."

"*Jah*, maybe, but you do what you have to do. Nurse first and then if they still seem hungry, we'll add a little formula. Do you want us to bathe them today?"

"*Nee*, maybe tomorrow. I keep them real clean."

"*Jah*, you sure do. You're a wonderful-*gut mudder*," Hazel said, nodding.

"I don't know how you do it," Martha added. "Five *kinner* is a lot all at once."

"What if I get in the family way again?" Deborah's eyes widened at the thought.

"You may have to take a breather," her sister said. "Surely, Eb would understand."

"I'm not too sure. He wants a big family."

"Well, then he'll have to do more to help," Hazel said, firmly. Martha nodded in agreement.

"Someone should talk to Paul about it, and maybe he can have a heart-to-heart talk with your husband," Martha stated.

"Even if he just held one of them when they're both crying, or watched the triplets for me when I'm tired."

Martha and Hazel exchanged glances. "We'll talk to him, too, if you want us to," Hazel said.

"Better not. He'll know we've been talking about him if you do. But Paul could try to get him to listen."

"Actually, I'll mention it to him this afternoon. He's not working today and he asked me to go for a buggy ride with him," Martha said. She looked over at Hazel, whose mouth was turned down. "If you can handle things for a little while without me, that is." How could she have forgotten Hazel and Paul were at one time serious about each other, and Hazel had admitted not being over him yet? She hadn't meant to hurt her new friend. Too late to take back the words.

"Oh, we'll be fine," Hazel said as she stood and walked over to the cribs. She patted Miriam.

"I made dinner already," Martha added, hoping that would help.

"I can smell it from up here," Deborah said. "It smells like chili."

"*Jah*, it is," Martha said. "I'd better go down and stir it. I'll serve it before I leave and we shouldn't be gone that long."

"Take as long as you please," Hazel said. "After all, pretty soon you'll be leaving, so we'd better get used to it."

Martha was afraid Hazel was upset, but surely just going for a buggy ride was not a terrible thing. Paul and she were merely friends.

Eventually, once they were able to get away from the house, Paul entertained her with stories of his *Rum-*

springa as his horse trotted along the road. When he was younger, Paul had traveled to New York City and spent three crazy days with two of his buddies.

Martha hadn't laughed that much in ages, and she loved his sense of humor. He liked to take pokes at himself and his friends, but he was never offensive, which she appreciated.

They went directly to the restaurant where they each ordered the chicken and dumplings. Then they had bread pudding for dessert along with coffee. They sat over an hour enjoying each other's company.

"This has been so relaxing, Paul. *Danki*. I didn't realize how much I've been stressed out. A lot of it is due to your dear friend, Ebenezer."

Paul's brows rose. "What happened?"

"That's just it. Nothing. The man is totally useless."

"Lots of men are. He takes care of his animals."

"Oh *jah*. But not his family! Poor Deborah does everything. She's exhausted. She's up half the night trying to care for her *boppli*."

"But Eb can't do much to help there," Paul offered.

Realizing he was referring to Deborah nursing her babies, she felt her face blush. "But he could change their diapers once in a while or watch his *sohns*, don't you think? I can't stay forever."

"No, I know." He turned his water glass, studying the melting ice. "Deb will miss you. We all will."

"But I need to get home. I might be able to stay another week or so, but it's a lot to put on Hazel after I leave. Plus, she's still needed at home."

"*Jah*, she's been *gut* about helping. Do you think I should have a talk with Eb? Maybe he doesn't realize how much he's needed."

"*Jah*, I wish you would talk to him about it. Make him understand she's worn out and anything he could do to help would be a blessing."

"Okay. When we get back, I'll take him aside. No guarantees, but I think he's really a *gut* person. Maybe a little on the lazy side, but he cares about his wife. I know that."

"Then he needs to chip in."

"I agree. You'd think he'd want to spend more time with the *kinner*. I can't wait to have kids of my own."

She smiled over. "I'm sorry we don't live closer, Paul. I really enjoy being with you."

"We're not that far apart. I could come visit you once in a while."

"*Jah* and, of course, I'll want to come visit here. I'll miss the *kinner* and Deborah."

"And?"

She giggled. "Okay, and you."

He reached across the table and patted her hand. Displays of affection amongst the Amish were rather rare—especially in public. Without a thought, she withdrew her hand and rested it on her lap, as she looked around to see if anyone was watching.

He quickly sat back and reached for his water glass. "Sorry," he muttered.

"*Nee*, I'm sorry. I didn't mean to react like that. I know you were just being friendly. Forgive me?"

His pout became a smile, and she noticed he had a dimple in his right cheek. Goodness, he was a looker.

After he paid the bill, they got back in the buggy. "Do you think we have time to go see my friend's garden?" he asked. "Our meal took longer than I expected."

Though it was tempting to spend more time with

Paul, she felt obligated to return home. Hazel had mentioned wanting to leave earlier than usual so she could stop at the market.

"I guess we'd better head back," she said reluctantly.

They rode back in silence except for the clopping of the horse's hooves against the paved road. Occasionally, he pulled over to the berm to allow a car to pass. Once they arrived, Paul came around and helped her down before securing the horse to a post.

As they walked back to the house, they could hear the wails of the babies coming from the kitchen. Eb came out of the barn and nodded as Martha walked past. Paul lagged behind. He went over to Eb, and as Martha continued walking to the house, she could hear them conversing in low tones. She was dying to know what they were saying, but she kept up her pace until she reached the kitchen.

When she came in, she found Hazel alone with the twins. They were in their car beds, which they now kept in the kitchen during the day for naps. Both were screaming.

As Hazel shook a baby bottle, she turned to Martha with a frazzled expression. "I'm so glad you're back. Deborah is finally napping. She's exhausted, but I've never made formula before and I did it wrong and had to start over again. Please try to stop one of the twins from screaming. I'm ready to scream myself."

Poor girl. Her hair had come loose from her *kapp* and she had spit-up on her shoulder.

Martha quickly lifted one of the girls—she wasn't sure which one—not that it mattered. Hazel handed her a full eight-ounce bottle and then began making a second one.

"You don't need so much milk, Hazel. They only take about two to three ounces."

"Oh, I had no idea. Well maybe we can pour some into another bottle and I won't make any more now."

They managed to pour half into the second bottle, and Hazel lifted the other baby out of the car bed and sat at the kitchen table across from Martha. "So how was your time with Paul?" she asked once the babies calmed down and tended to their bottles.

"It was nice. He's very polite."

"*Jah*. I think he likes you. Do you like him?"

"As a friend, *jah*. That's all."

"He's nice looking, don't you think?"

"Pretty nice."

"I hope Deborah sleeps a while. She was real teary again. I think she's depressed."

"Baby blues, the English call it."

"Did you have a chance to talk to Paul about Eb?"

"*Jah*. They may be talking now. He was very willing to do it."

"I figured. If *you* asked him."

"He knows Eb is lazy, but he can't understand why he isn't more interested in his own *kinner*."

Hazel nodded. "I know Paul really likes *kinner*. I'd hoped we'd have a big family together. Oh well, I guess the *gut* Lord has someone else in mind for me."

"Maybe you'd like my friend Daniel Beiler. Why don't you come visit me when things settle down, and I'll introduce you to him."

"Was he the boyfriend?"

"Ex-boyfriend. I think."

"You think?"

A little boy's voice came from the living room. Then Luke let out a holler. "Leave it alone! It's my ball!"

Martha stood up and keeping the bottle in the baby's mouth, she made her way into the living room. "You *buwe* were playing so nicely for a while, I thought you'd fallen asleep."

Matthew and Mark giggled. "We were just being *gut* for a change," Mark said.

"Well, if you continue, maybe I'll bake some cookies when I'm done feeding your *schwester*, and maybe you can help."

"Chocolate chip?" Luke asked, looking over wide-eyed.

"Sure. I think I saw a bag of chips. No promises though. You all three have to be very, very *gut* the rest of the afternoon. Your *mamm* is trying to sleep."

"Let's take the ball outside and play," Luke suggested and the three boys took off for the yard.

About an hour later, Hazel left for home and then Paul came into the house. Deborah and the babies were sleeping, so Martha found herself alone with Paul. She couldn't wait to hear about his talk with Eb.

Chapter Twelve

"How did it go?" Martha asked Paul, as she dried her hands on a terry hand towel. They sat down at the table adjacent to each other.

"I think it went pretty *gut*. He said he didn't realize how tired Deborah was, and he agreed to watch the boys more now."

"I hope he follows through. The poor girl is totally wore out."

"He said he was glad for your help. I thought you'd want to know that."

"*Jah*, I guess. I wouldn't have guessed it by the way he talks to me."

"I think you're wonderful to help like you do. It's not like you're close to Deborah. I mean you two didn't know each other real *gut* before, did you?"

"Not really, but I like helping people when I can. My *mudder* is the same way. We often visit the sick together. She bakes a lot and takes goodies to everyone."

"That's real nice. Do you like to cook?"

"It's okay. I'm not real *gut* yet, but I'm getting better,

I think. My *daed* teases me about my pies, though. The crusts are kinda sloppy looking, next to my *mudder*'s."

Paul smiled and nodded. "My oldest sister hates making pies, but her cakes are the best. Especially her spice cake. I'll have to have you meet my family next time we go out together—which I hope will be soon."

"Oh, I doubt I'll be able to play hooky again. At least for a while."

"How much longer will you be staying? Do you know?"

"I'm waiting to hear from my family. I suggested staying another week, so if that works out, I have three more weeks here."

He nodded. "I'm sure we'll get some alone time then."

Now that sounded like he was getting serious. She wished she had a better idea of where she stood with Daniel. She should write to her friend Naomi and see if he was still taking Molly home from the Singings. Naomi would tell her the truth.

It was difficult to find the time or the energy to write to anyone, but before she'd allow herself to start thinking about starting a relationship with Paul, she needed to be sure things were final with Daniel. It was strange. She really didn't care if it was over, so obviously, she wasn't in love with the man.

That should be enough of an answer to her question. In fact, it shouldn't matter how he feels about her anymore, if indeed there was no love on her part.

"Hey, you look like you're a million miles away. Am I that boring?"

Martha let out a laugh. "Goodness, you're not boring at all. I was just thinking about home."

"And a certain someone?" he asked.

"How on earth did you figure that out?" she asked.

"Oh, I read minds, didn't I tell you?"

She shook her head. "Guess I forgot. So what am I thinking now?"

"That you want to spend more time with me; that I'm the nicest guy you ever met; that we—"

"Whoa! Where's your Amish humility?"

"Oops, I left it at home."

Eb came in the door at that moment and nodded over at the two of them. "Thought I'd go see how Deborah's doing? Think she's awake yet?"

Martha smiled widely. "It doesn't matter, Eb. I think she'd be delighted to see you. Are the *buwe* okay? We can go sit outside and watch them."

"*Jah.* I was playing ball with them, but I want to check upstairs now."

Paul rose, followed by Martha, and they went out together. Then Paul went into their play area and threw the ball around with the boys, who caught one out of fifty throws.

Martha decided to sit and watch. He sure was good with children. He was so patient. A nice quality. And how nice to have someone she could joke around with. With Daniel, everything was serious. Ugh. Molly could have him. It was time for Martha to consider an alternative. Yes, Paul was a special person. Maybe she'd come every month for a few days—to help Deborah and Eb, of course.

Naomi Shoemaker tucked the letter she'd written to Martha into her mailbox and lifted the flag for the mailman. Then she walked back to the baby carriage and pushed her sister, Patty, back to the front porch where she decided to take a few minutes to enjoy the pleasant breeze. It had cooled off considerably from the day before, and even though she'd prefer to live in a town, it was a pleasant view from their glider on the front porch.

She left the sleeping baby in the carriage, after making sure the child was shaded from the sun, and sat on the glider, shifting it back and forth with her feet, as she tucked a loose strand of hair under her *kapp*. What a boring summer so far. Why did her mother keep having babies, if she ended up making her children do all the work?

When Martha got back maybe she'd talk to her about going away for a weekend sometime with her. She had no idea where they'd go, but how nice it would be to have a change of scenery and not have to wash diapers every single day. Surely, between her aunts and her sisters, she could get a break. It just wasn't fair.

As she sat on the porch, two of her younger brothers came out of the house with brooms. "We have to sweep the porch, so you'd better move," said twelve-year-old Tommy with a tone of authority.

"We can sweep around her," Bruce, who was a year younger, suggested.

"I'll get up and move. Just let me wheel Patty away so she doesn't get leaves all over her."

"No leaves yet, just dust."

"Then dust. That's not any better."

She pushed the carriage around to the back of the house. Her mother called out the kitchen door. "You'd better get those diapers out while we still have sun."

"*Jah*, I will."

"You can leave the *boppli* in the carriage. I have to

weed the garden so I'll watch her while you bring the diapers out to the line."

"Okay," Naomi responded automatically. *Borrrring.* She decided right then and there, she'd never marry. Never! Even teaching would be better than this.

It was amazing! The next few days Eb was a totally different man. He watched, and even played with his three sons every afternoon, allowing Deborah to nap or care for the twins without distraction. He still fished most early mornings, but then he'd clean the fish and sometimes even grill them rather than expect someone else to cook them. He even smiled once in a while and lo and behold, Martha caught him holding one of the twins when she cried one evening. Too bad someone hadn't addressed the issue earlier. It might have saved poor Deborah a lot of tears.

Paul was back working, but still managed to come around almost every evening. He and Martha took walks around the yard and once he reached for her hand, but she wasn't comfortable yet to take their relationship to the next level, though she found herself thinking about him more and more and looked forward to his arrival each evening.

Hazel spent at least three or four hours every day helping and she and Martha had become good friends. Nothing more was said about Paul, but Hazel mentioned a young man who had paid attention to her at the church service, and Martha noted her eyes lit up when she talked about him.

Martha's parents had given her the okay to remain a week longer if she was needed, much to everyone's delight—especially Paul's. They agreed to try to see each other at least once a month after she went back home, and since he was earning money, it was decided he would do the bulk of the travel. When he checked with the driver he knew, he was told it was only about a hundred-mile drive, which they could do in about two hours.

Martha had not even mentioned him to her family, but the last time she wrote she told them she had made a new friend. She even used his name, though she made it sound as if it was strictly a platonic friendship. Whether her parents read more into it, she wasn't able to determine from their response.

The twins had finally settled into a routine and the dark circles under Deborah's eyes had all but disappeared. She seemed over her depression and began taking an interest in the normal routines, even taking over some of the meals. With only a week left for Martha to be there to help, it was a relief on everyone's part. Eb still took a keener interest in his family.

While they were folding the dried diapers one afternoon in the kitchen, Deborah talked about her desire to be a better housekeeper. "It helped that you got things organized for me," she said to Martha. "I guess I'd given up somewhere along the line."

"Well, you were also real pregnant. That didn't make it any easier."

"That was just an excuse, I'm afraid. It was more depression, now that I look back. I was so discouraged about Eb not taking any interest in the *kinner*. Or me."

"He has really changed."

"*Jah*, thanks to Paul having that talk with him. Eb told me last night he was sorry he didn't help out more. He just thought I liked doing everything, I guess."

"Some Amish women do like it better when their husbands don't get involved, I suppose. Not me. I want my husband to be a real part of raising the *kinner* when I have them."

"Speaking about husbands—what's the story with Paul?"

"No story, really. We're just friends."

"Maybe on your part, but I think he's smitten with you."

"We live a distance."

"Not that far. Maybe too far for a buggy, but with a car…"

"True. We are going to try to get together every month or so. Maybe oftener."

"I'm glad. He's such a nice man, Martha. I hope you'll end up together."

"My biggest problem would be if I had to move away and leave my parents. I'm their only child, you know. It would be real hard on them."

"Tell him if it starts getting serious. He'd probably be willing to move to your area. You said it was only about a hundred miles away. He could visit his family over holidays and all."

"You're getting way ahead of things, Deborah," Martha said, smiling over. "Now let me go check and see if the towels are dry yet. There's such a nice breeze today."

"Oh, I'm going to miss you, dear friend."

"And I, you," Martha said. She patted the top of Deborah's *kapp* as she walked back out to the clothesline. "I hear some arguing with the *buwe*. I'll stop and sort that out while I'm there."

"And I'd better check the *maedel*. It's time for them to be waking up."

Chapter Thirteen

Martha, Deborah, and Hazel spent the following week scrubbing, organizing, and discarding anything unnecessary from Deborah's house, making it easier for her to keep things under control. They hoped it would set her on the path to good housekeeping. They sang together some of the church songs they knew by heart, and made it a joyful time rather than the drudgery some might consider it. The boys responded by being more obedient. Even the twins took solid naps at the same time, which made it ever so much easier.

Each evening, Paul headed over to the house and even when Martha would have preferred to relax and do nothing, she would instead go for a buggy ride or a walk around the property. With only three days left before Martha was scheduled to leave, Paul and she were well aware of their upcoming separation, and what it might mean for their budding relationship. Paul said he'd try to come for a visit after she was back home a couple of weeks.

Autumn was fast approaching and Paul mentioned he'd be needed by his father for the harvest. In spite of what lay ahead, he assured Martha he'd visit fairly frequently. Since he'd have the evenings free during the mid-week, and the help of his three brothers, the harvest should go well. His father was still actively in charge and even with three farms to clear, Paul did not anticipate a problem.

"I'd like you to come for supper tomorrow," he mentioned as they stood at the horse stable to pat the horses.

"*Jah*? Does your *mamm* know?"

"I mentioned it to her this morning. She wants to meet you before you go back."

"So, you've told your family about me?"

"Not everything," he said with a crooked smile, "but they know I'm not home much and they suspected it was a woman."

She grinned. "The word 'woman' makes me feel so old."

"You're twenty. That makes you a woman."

"Still…"

He reached for her hand and held it in both of his. "I really care for you a lot."

"I know. Me, too."

"Would you be upset if I kissed you?"

Her heart began beating wildly. "I… I guess it would be okay. One time."

He drew her into his strong arms and she could feel his breath on her cheek as he searched for her lips with his. His eyes were closed. She liked the smell of peppermint on his breath and the feel of his embrace. Hopefully, her heart would remain in place and he wouldn't be aware of her nervousness. She remained absolutely still while he pressed his lips upon hers. It was over in an instant, but somehow that simple kiss changed the equation entirely. They were no longer just friends. A line had been crossed.

Paul stepped back but ran his hands down her arms reaching for her hands. "You're very sweet."

"*Danki.*" She hesitated before adding, "I'm glad we'll see each other again soon."

"*Jah*, me, too. I wish we had phones," he added.

"Me, too. Some of my friends have phones, but they hide them from their parents."

"Would you be able to do that?"

"I… I don't know," she said hesitantly. "It might make me feel too guilty."

"But maybe you could use your friend's phone. I would buy one, if I knew we could talk once in a while, but I won't ask you to do anything that would make you feel guilty. After all, we can write to each other."

Martha nodded. "I think that would be better. I'll write you every week."

"Not every day?"

She grinned. "Depends."

"Upon?"

"Will I hear back from you more than once a week?"

"*Jah.* For sure."

"Promise?"

"I promise. Maybe not every day, but at least every other day. I'll even seal it with another kiss." He began to lean over with his eyes closed, but she drew back.

"*Nee.* Once is enough, Paul."

He opened his eyes wide. "Did you not like it?"

"I liked it. Maybe too much," she admitted, speaking softly now as she avoided his eyes.

"Then I'm okay with your rejection." He dropped her

hands and placed his forefinger under her chin. "You can look at me now."

Her eyes turned up and she felt a flush on her cheeks. He sure was handsome.

"We'll go back in now," he said. "It's getting cool out here for you. I love this time of year."

As they headed back, Eb appeared with a pile of old Budget newspapers. "Headed to the burn pile. Guess if it's not windy, I'll get rid of the trash tomorrow. That wife of mine has more trash every day."

"*Jah*, we're cleaning up real *gut*," Martha said, as she and Paul stopped to talk.

"*Danki* for helping out," Eb managed to say. He was a man of few words and she knew it was an effort for him to actually thank her.

"I was glad to help. I'll still come sometimes to lend a hand. I've gotten close to your little ones, Eb."

"*Jah*. I guess." He turned and walked off with his filled arms as Martha and Paul finished their walk back to the kitchen door. They avoided holding hands if others were present, but it was no secret that their relationship was more than friendship.

The next evening, Paul picked her up a little earlier and took her to his home where his mother was preparing a supper of cold cuts and salads. She had also baked cobbler for dessert.

She was older-looking than her husband, but she had been a pretty woman in her youth and still had an engaging smile. There were no hugs exchanged, but his parents were both cordial and saw to it that she had plenty to eat.

Martha found it difficult to chew her food in front of his family and she ate very little supper, though she was able to get down a full serving of cobbler. Paul's older siblings, three brothers and two sisters, each with several children stopped by during the course of the evening. Martha tried desperately to remember their names, but it was too difficult a task. Mercy. She wasn't used to such a large family. They were rather a quiet family, but pleasant enough. She noticed they didn't display physical affection towards each other, but many of the Amish she knew were the same. Her small family was the exception and she was quite glad. Now Paul, she felt, was more like she was, which she would require in a mate. If she was willing, he'd probably hold her hand all the time.

The afternoon she left, it was difficult to say goodbye to everyone when the car drew up to return her to Lancaster County. Paul had not attempted to kiss Martha again, and secretly, she was somewhat disappointed, but she would never initiate something so personal.

As she pulled away, the whole family, plus Paul and Hazel, stood watching and waving. She felt slight apprehension when she watched Hazel move next to Paul before they were out of sight. Even though Paul had told her it was off between them, she knew—as only a woman knows—Hazel still had feelings for him. Well, there was nothing she could do about it. She'd just write often and visit when it was possible. While she couldn't be certain that Paul was the man she would one day marry, she felt in her heart that he might well be the one. The one thing she was confident about were her feelings for Daniel. What she felt at this point were definitely feelings of friendship and nothing more.

She sat back and closed her eyes. Her mind was transitioning, and she now looked forward to seeing her parents again. She just hoped her mother had not become too exhausted without her there to help. It was a sacrifice on her mother's part to spare her daughter for that length of time, since she was not a strong woman. Probably weakened from her bout with cancer years before.

Martha prayed silently for those she was leaving and those she was returning to. The only name absent from her prayers was Daniel Beiler, though when she realized she had neglected him entirely, she added a word for his health. How life changes.

Chapter Fourteen

"Now Sarah, sit down. You're giving me the jitters, pacing the way you are. Martha will be home soon and you gettin' all nervous about it won't bring her here one minute sooner."

"I expected her an hour ago. I hope there hasn't been an accident or—"

"Settle down. Maybe we should go for a walk. Get your mind off it."

"I'm much too wore out, Melvin. I scrubbed down the walls in Martha's room this morning so it would smell nice and fresh for her. And of course, I made her favorite cookies."

"I thought you were making them for me," he said with a smile.

"Well, I made a double batch, that's for sure. Put extra butterscotch chips in, too."

"Maybe I should test them out first."

She shook her head and pretended to be annoyed. "I know you, you'll stick a bunch in your pocket."

"I think I hear a car." He walked over to the front window of the sitting room. "Sure enough. Here she comes."

"Oh, I'm so relieved. Let's go outside to greet her."

They went out the front door and stood waiting for the driver to stop at the house. Their driver, Hank Hudson, popped the trunk as Martha quickly opened the car door and ran over to her parents. They encircled each other with their arms. Sarah had tears in her eyes.

"Let me pay Hank and then we'll hear all about your stay," Melvin said, breaking away and reaching in his pocket for the money.

"Your daughter looks real rosy-cheeked," Hank remarked. "Think the vacation agreed with her."

"Oh, it was no vacation," Sarah said upon hearing his remark. "My Martha was there to help. She's my angel girl. Always doing for others."

"Oh, *Mamm*, don't brag. You're embarrassing me."

The driver chuckled. "I guess even you Amish can be proud once in a while."

Melvin shook his head. "Don't report us, Hank. Your tip will go down next time."

Everyone laughed and after leaving off her luggage, the driver took off and the three of them went into the house, her father carrying her belongings. Martha and her mother kept their arms around each other's waists, and even Martha had to wipe her eyes. How lucky she was to have such loving parents.

"You'll be happy to hear that Daniel Beiler and his parents are coming for supper tonight. He couldn't wait for you to come home."

Martha stopped walking. Her mouth dropped open. "But he never even wrote! What makes him think we're still…you know…caring about each other?"

Melvin turned to his daughter. "That boy came by every couple days, and we read your letters to him. He's still smitten, Martha. Don't you worry none. We'll hear wedding bells pretty soon, for sure. Most guys just don't like to write letters."

"Oh, this is awful."

"Honey, what do you mean?" her mother asked, her lips turned down.

"I... I... Oh, it's okay. It will work out alright. Just don't seat us together and please don't invite him over again, without checking with me first."

"You sure don't sound like a future bride—talking that way." Her father shook his head and then made his way upstairs to her room with the suitcase.

"Did that young man you told us about in your letters— Paul something—put ideas in your head?" her mother asked, lowering her voice. "He was Amish, no?"

"*Jah*, he's a *gut* Amishman. We are *gut* friends, that's for certain."

"And that's all?"

"I think so."

"That don't sound so positive."

"I hear *Daed* coming back down. Maybe we can talk later. Don't worry, I won't be rude to Daniel, but I actually thought he didn't care anymore. I'm shocked."

"He's a little odd, Martha. Rather a moody young man, but I think he's an honest sort and certainly a hard worker."

"I need more, *Mamm*. A lot more."

Melvin arrived in the kitchen where the women were settling down at the table. The cookies were already on a plate.

"Where's the *kaffi*, Sarah?"

"It's brewing. I put it on before Martha even arrived. Don't you smell it?"

"Guess I do. I'll get the milk."

"Already in a pitcher in the refrigerator."

"I found out that I don't make very *gut kaffi*," Martha said, grinning at her parents.

"No big secret to brewing *kaffi*," Sarah said. "Just always add an extra scoop for the pot. My *Mamm* taught me that."

"How are *Mammi* and *Dawdi*? I've missed them, too."

"They're doing real *gut*. They should be heading over soon to see you. Your *Dawdi* probably ain't up from his nap quite yet."

Melvin checked his watch and then placed three cookies on the placemat in front of him.

"I'm so glad you made butterscotch cookies, *Mamm*. My favorite."

"Looks like your *Daed*'s favorite as well," Sarah added, smiling over at her husband.

"Your *Mamm*'s been starving me since you've been away."

"Oh right," Sarah said. "That's why your trousers are so tight. I may have to put a patch in the waistline."

"I think you both look *wunderbaar*," Martha said as the back door opened and her grandparents came in. Martha went over and embraced her grandmother, and her grandfather grinned and patted her on the head.

"You look *gut*, Martha," he added. "Little tired in the eyes though."

"I haven't slept much, *Dawdi*. The *boppli* woke me every time they wanted to be fed."

"That young *maed* sure has her hands full," he added. "How were the triplets? *Gut*?"

"Better by the time I left. They sure were an unruly bunch when I first got there. Deborah's *schwester*, Hazel, came nearly every day to help out. She's gonna be there for Deborah, I'm sure of that."

"I don't remember the family that well. I guess it's been about ten years since we've seen them." Sarah sipped at her coffee and broke a cookie in half, placing half on Martha's placemat and taking the rest for herself.

"I want to go back frequently to lend a hand," Martha said.

"That's real nice of you," her father said, nodding.

Sarah looked over with a solemn expression. Martha wondered if her mother was thinking of another attraction in Lewistown.

In fact, Sarah had major concerns. If her daughter became serious with someone two hours away by car, how often would they see each other? And when the grandchildren arrived, how much help could she be that far away? She'd try to encourage Martha to accept Daniel's offer of marriage, when it came. Surely, it would, since Daniel was already twenty-four, with a birthday coming up in the fall. He'd want to get started with a family, and surely Martha would be anxious as well.

Mammi and *Dawdi* sat at the table and Sarah rose to add more mugs. Then she poured their coffee and replaced the pot on the stove to stay hot.

"Lizzy is coming by tomorrow. I guess I told you, didn't I?" *Mammi* asked, turning to her daughter.

"*Nee*, you didn't," Sarah responded.

"*Ach*, I guess now I am. I need to get started on that quilt. So how about if the four of us go into town to pick out the fabrics. And you need to decide on the pattern, Martha. I'm not as quick at sewing as I used to be."

"I'll certainly help," Sarah said.

"*Jah*, I figured you would."

"I may not be as *gut* at quilting as my *schwester*, but I want to be part of it."

"That's why I want you to come along tomorrow, Sarah. It will be fun for us all to be together. Maybe I'll treat to lunch."

"Now ain't that nice," Melvin said.

His father-in-law nodded in agreement. "Just leave something for us menfolk to eat."

"There should be leftovers you can eat," *Mammi* suggested.

"Humph."

"What are you making for tonight?" *Mammi* asked Sarah. "I know you have the Beilers coming."

"It's just supper, so I made cole slaw, potato salad, and we have our bologna and sauerbraten left from the noon dinner."

"I've missed your sauerbraten, *Mamm*," Martha said. "No one cooks it like you do."

Sarah sat a little taller and shook her head. "Oh, I'm not that *gut*."

"Oh, *jah*, you are," her husband said in her defense. "Why do you think I married you?"

Everyone laughed and then the subject returned to the quilt.

"*Mammi*," Martha began, "there's no big rush about the quilt. No date has been set and I'm not sure there will be."

Mammi's mouth dropped open. "My goodness gracious! I thought it was a sure thing."

Sarah shook her head. "Apparently, we read it wrong, *Mamm*."

"Well, that young man better pick up speed or he'll lose our sweet *maed* to someone else."

"He already may have," Sarah let slip. Everyone became silent and Melvin finally commented.

"What's this all about?"

"Oh, *Daed*, there's nothing to tell you at this point. Okay, I have a new friend and maybe I like him, but it's more the fact that Daniel is so serious about everything. He's not fun to be with."

"Fun? Since when does a man have to be fun? Ain't it enough if he knows how to farm *gut* and be faithful to *Gott* and his family? What's this fun thing?"

"Now, Melvin, Martha wants to enjoy her life and if her husband goes around with a long face all the time and can't even be cheerful, that sure don't sound like a *gut* marriage."

"Well, I'm no comedian, and we seem to have gotten along okay all these years."

"But you smile at me a lot, in private anyway, and you're nice to be around. Not grouchy that much."

"Hmm. Didn't know it mattered."

"Oh, it matters," *Mammi* added with a nod. "Me and my husband know how to have a *gut* laugh sometimes. We even know how to laugh at ourselves."

"*Jah*, which is pretty often," *Dawdi* added, grinning over.

"So I guess I kinda lost that argument," Melvin said, turning his mug around while giving it his full attention.

"We sure weren't arguing about anything," Sarah said defensively. "Just have a different way of seeing things sometimes, I guess."

"Well, our *dochder* will make up her own mind about things, that's for sure," Melvin added. "That's the way *maedel* are these days. Not like the old times. Now pass the plate of cookies, if you please," he said grimacing at his wife.

Martha glanced at the clock. The company wouldn't arrive for another hour, leaving her time to write a quick note to Paul—and one to Deborah, of course. She excused herself and went upstairs for privacy. No point in mentioning anything about the supper plans to her friends back in Lewistown. Just not that important.

Chapter Fifteen

Martha licked the envelope and sealed her letter to Paul. She had ended up writing over six pages and hadn't even begun a letter to Deborah. She did mention in Paul's, that she would be writing to Deborah soon, and in the meantime, to give them all her love when he saw them. She wondered if he'd still come around each evening as he had while she was living there. Somehow, she doubted it.

After glancing in the small square framed mirror above her dresser, she noted her hair was escaping from the *kapp*. She removed it and brushed out her waist-length tresses. She wondered who in the family she'd gotten the dark hair from. Nearly all her relatives were blonde with blue eyes. Her thick hair was nearly black and it had a gleam as she brushed it. She was secretly pleased with her appearance and even liked having dark brown eyes along with long lashes which curved all on their own.

A buggy turned down the drive and she guessed it was the Beiler's. *Jah*, and then a second buggy turned in with some of the older children. There were eight altogether and another on the way. You'd expect a lot of gabbing and spirited discussions, but they were a quiet group, very proper in dress and behavior. Some might say boring, but Martha avoided that conclusion.

She quickly tied her hair up in a bun and replaced her *kapp*, which barely contained the mass of hair.

When she came down the stairs, the Beilers were already gathered in the sitting room. The younger children sat on the floor as the adults took the comfortable seating. When she entered the room, Daniel stood and nodded. "Hi."

"*Hallo*," she said, including the whole family in her greeting.

There were some "*hallo*s" returned to her and two of his sisters smiled pleasantly.

"So how was your trip?" Mrs. Beiler asked with an expressionless face.

"It was nice. I was very busy though."

"*Jah*, I'd know about that," Daniel's mother responded. "*Kinner* are lots of work."

"*Jah*," Martha said.

"What did they name the twins?"

Martha told them and then since it was so quiet in the room, she added the names of the triplets to make conversation. Then she gave their ages and tried to think of anything that might interest the family. It was difficult.

Sarah joined in and asked Rebecca, Daniel's mother, how she was feeling.

"Tired, most of the time."

"I can imagine."

"You only had the one. You have no idea."

"Well, I've been around big families all my life."

"Not the same."

"I guess not."

"Martha, do you want to help me pour the water? The supper is just about ready," Sarah said.

"About time. I'm starving," Thomas, Daniel's father, announced.

Martha looked over to see if he was joking. He wasn't. Oh dear. She followed her mother into the kitchen and filled a water pitcher from the sink. Her mother looked over and lifted her eyebrows. "Not big at talk, are they?" she asked softly.

"See what I mean?" Martha responded in even lower tones.

Once the water was poured and the assorted salads set around the table on platters, Martha went back to the sitting room and asked their guests to join them for supper.

After everyone was seated, Melvin led the grace in silence and then the eating began. No one spoke except to ask for more food. No comments were made about the supper. Martha noticed her mother had not set out the sauerbraten and she smiled to herself. *Jah*, her *mamm* was saving it for her. Why waste it on people who wouldn't appreciate the work that went into it.

After the meal, the men and boys went out to the barn with Melvin and the women and girls congregated in the kitchen to clean up. With so many hands, it went quickly, which was a relief to Martha. She couldn't wait for the night to end. As she set her damp dishtowel on a rack, Daniel appeared at the back door. He opened it and nodded to everyone.

"I thought you'd like to take a walk with me," he said directly to Martha.

She looked over at her mother, who gave a faint nod.

"Sure, but I'm real tired and I'll probably only walk for a couple of minutes."

"That's fine."

He held the door open for her and then followed her out. They walked around one of the corn fields, barely speaking. Finally, she stopped and put her hands on her hips. He looked slightly baffled as she stood before him. He removed his straw hat and twirled it between his hands. "Are you okay?" he asked.

"I'm just a little confused. My parents told me you came by frequently while I was gone, yet you never even sent me a note. I figured things were over between us."

"I have no idea why you'd think that. I never said I was through."

"*Nee*, but it was rather obvious. I know you took Molly Zook home from the Singings a couple times."

"Only because she needed a ride. Her older *bruder* left her each time so he could take his girl home."

"Still, you've acted pretty strange with me. I just don't get it."

"I haven't changed my mind. I want us to be married someday."

"Well, I'm not so sure anymore."

His eyes stared in disbelief. "Why not?"

"I don't want to hurt you, Daniel, but I don't think I love you."

"Well, I'm not head over heels myself, but I think we'd make a *gut* couple. I think you're a *gut* woman with high morals and our *kinner* would be nice looking and *schmaert* enough—at least that's what I think."

"But there has to be love."

"Not necessarily. My *daed* said he didn't love my

mudder too much when they married, and look at them now."

"I do. They don't seem particularly happy."

"There's more to life than being 'happy' you know. They have a *gut* family. There is control in our home. You can see that for yourself. And it's not like I don't care about you. I do. I would try to make you comfortable. I work hard and I'm a pretty *gut* farmer, if I do say so myself. You would never starve."

"*Gut* grief. What a thing to say."

"I'm curious, Sarah. Did you meet a man while you were gone? Your one letter mentioned a Paul Yoder. Did you fancy him or something?"

"He's a very nice man, Daniel, but there is nothing between us."

"I'm glad to hear that. I fully intend to win your hand in marriage, Martha. I think you just got upset when you thought I had another girl I was interested in. You can stop being mad at me now that you know the truth."

"I wasn't mad."

"*Jah*, I think you were. You even look mad now."

"Oh, you frustrate me, Daniel. You don't hear a word I'm saying. I'll try to make it clear. It's over between us."

"*Nee*, I don't believe that for a second." He moved towards her, put his hat back on his head and put his hands on her shoulders. "I won't give up. I care too much to just let you go, and I know you must still care for me. Maybe you even loved me. You can love me again. You just have to see more of me."

"No. I don't want you to come by again."

"Martha, Martha. Listen to you. You sound like a child scorned." Before she could say a word, he pulled her forward and kissed her soundly on her mouth.

She pushed with all her might and turned and ran towards the house. She could hear him laughing behind her. "The lady doth protest too much," he called after her.

She wiped her mouth with her hand. Hate suddenly filled her heart. She knew it was wrong. It was a sin to hate, but that's what she felt. How dare he? She felt defiled. If he came by again, she'd consider leaving the area permanently until he found another woman to control. Of course, how could she leave her beloved parents? Should she tell her mother what happened? Would her parents stand behind her? She knew the answer immediately. They'd do anything for her. Their love was unconditional. Just like her Jesus.

Hot tears flowed as she went through the front door so she could go to her room without being seen by the Beilers. When she got to her room, she pushed a chair against the door and laid on her bed and wept.

"Oh, Paul, I wish you were here. You'd protect me from that monster. Oh, thank goodness, I'm not marrying him. What a horrible marriage that would have been."

Eventually, she heard the two buggies pull out of the drive. She knew her mother would want to find out what happened, but not tonight. It was no lie to tell her she had a headache. When her mother knocked on her bedroom door, Martha announced her head problem. Her mother told her she'd pray for her and she wouldn't have to get up early the next morning, but she should rest instead.

After her mother's footsteps were no longer heard, Martha closed her eyes and eventually fell asleep, though she had horrible dreams—nightmares of living with Daniel and having a houseful of angry little children. Oh, she'd rather remain single forever.

Chapter Sixteen

It felt strange to be at Eb and Deborah Lapp's house without the lovely smiling Martha there to greet him. At first Paul thought he'd skip even stopping this evening, but if Eb needed help, he wanted to be there for him. Besides, it was lonely at his own home now that his three older brothers and two older sisters were all married. His father had plenty of help with the farm from the family, since everyone lived within a mile of the family homestead, so he wasn't worried about his father overworking, if he didn't show up.

The day had gone well, even though he had trouble getting Martha off his mind. He and his boss had installed kitchen cabinets they'd completed, and the owners were so pleased with the results, they gave them each fifty dollars extra. That's a rarity and much appreciated. Paul set aside as much money every week as he could, after giving some to his parents for his room and board. He wanted to buy his own place, and now since he'd met Martha Troyer, he was even more determined to buy a home.

Deborah handed one of the twins to Eb and Paul offered to hold the other one, so she could put the boys to bed. There were tears galore as the boys fought physically with each other. Finally, Eb stepped in and punished them. Once they quieted down, Deborah marched them upstairs and led them to the bathroom to prepare for the night.

Eb looked down at his twin daughter, Miriam, and grinned. "She looks like her *mudder*, don't you think?"

"Honestly? I don't see any resemblance to anyone yet. *Boppli* are *boppli*, though I'll admit they're pretty cute. Can you tell them apart?"

"*Nee*, but don't tell Deborah. I wait for her to name them before I say anything. I bet you miss Martha, don't you?"

"I'd be lying if I said no. She's become pretty special to me, Eb."

"I could tell."

"Do you think she likes me at all?"

"Come on, stop playing games. You know she does. She always has a special smile for you. She's pretty *gut* looking, if you ask me."

"*Schmaert*, too."

"Maybe that's important. I don't know. As long as a *maed* could cook and clean, I didn't care how *gut* they were in their brains."

"I like a woman who can talk about things other than *kinner*," Paul continued. "Martha even knows about politics. Can you believe it?"

"That's a hard one. I don't even follow that."

"And she's *gut* with history, too. We have nice talks about the martyrs sometimes and even about the Revolutionary War."

"I guess I learned all that stuff in school, but I don't

remember much. You were always the schmaert guy in our class."

"I liked learning things. Sometimes I wish we Amish were allowed to go on to finish high school and even on to college."

"You're a *gut* carpenter, Paul. What more do you need to know about?"

"I guess. Anyway, they don't allow it, so there's not much to think about. I sure don't want to leave the community."

"I could never leave. This is the way I want to spend my life." Mariam woke up and began to cry. "Uh-oh, I bet she's hungry. I'll take her up to Deborah so she can feed her."

"You may as well get your *buwe* to bed then, don't you think?" Paul asked nonchalantly.

"I guess," he answered, with a slight pout forming. "Sure, why not?"

Paul sat on the sofa and looked down at the sleeping Mary. She sure was cute. What would his children look like? Would they be blonde like him or would they take after their mother and have dark features and hair? Whoa! He was sure getting ahead of himself. But if they ended up loving each other, and she was agreeable, he'd like to marry within a year. After all, it was going to be hard living two hours apart by car. If it was to work out for them, it would mean he'd have to make a real effort to keep their relationship growing, and you couldn't do that if you didn't see much of each other.

He ran his finger along the baby's cheek. So soft. Deborah kept the babies changed and they always smelled of talcum powder or Ivory Soap. He was sure Martha would be every bit as good a mother. There was just nothing that she wouldn't be good at—that was for sure.

Back in Paradise, the morning came too quickly for Martha. She'd had so many unpleasant dreams, she didn't feel rested at six when she normally rose. It was quiet in the house, which was the norm, since she was their only child—and an adult at that. She dozed off again and when she finally did rise, she was shocked to see it was nearly nine o'clock.

After dressing in one of her nicer dresses, she went downstairs to find her mother preparing four loaves of bread. She looked over and smiled at her daughter. "You look nice. I hope you feel rested."

"I guess I will eventually. Right now, that *kaffi* smells real *gut*."

"Can I make you some oatmeal?"

"*Nee, danki*, I'll just have a piece of toast with some of your marmalade on it. I've been craving your orange marmalade ever since I left." Martha reached for her familiar green mug and poured herself some coffee.

"I should have sent some along with you. That was thoughtless of me. I'm sorry."

"Oh, *Mamm*, don't apologize. I didn't mean to make you feel bad. Deborah's *mudder* brought some strawberry jam for us. It wasn't bad at all." She sat at the table and watched as her mother turned one of the future loaves of bread and kneaded it. Since she was so used to baking her own bread, it was almost automatic. "I think I'll turn one of these loaves into cinnamon raisin bread. I know how much you love it."

"Oh wow! I can't wait."

There was a quick rap on the kitchen door and *Mammi* opened it up and poked her head in.

Sarah looked over at her mother. "*Mamm*, come on in. Why the knock?" she asked.

"I didn't want to come in if you were talking about me," she said as she grinned at her granddaughter.

Martha giggled as she shook her head. "I slept in, *Mammi*, and I'm still just waking up."

"Goodness, that's not like you! They worked my darling girl too hard, I'm thinking."

"*Nee*, I didn't sleep *gut* though. Too many thoughts popping around my head."

"Oh, I hate nights like that. Want to share your poppings?"

"Not today. I just want to enjoy my family."

"Your *Aenti* Lizzy should be here in about an hour. You ladies didn't forget I'm treating for lunch, did you? I'll take you to that place with the homemade ice cream."

"Sounds *gut*, *Mammi*," Martha said. "I hope they have peanut butter swirl."

"I like their raisin rum," Sarah said, running her tongue over her upper lip in anticipation.

"And are you okay with picking out your fabric, Martha? Even if there ain't a real need for it yet?" her grandmother asked.

"Sure. Would the Carpenter's Stars pattern be too hard, *Mammi*?"

"Not at all. I made one for my best friend when she got married. That was a long time ago, but I think I still have the pattern somewhere. If not, I'll pick up another one. Have you thought about the colors?"

"Not really, but I love greens and pinks together. I'll wait till we go to the store and maybe I'll get inspired."

Her mother nodded. "There's a lot of work in that pattern. I've never helped make one, but if you tell me what to do, *Mamm*, I can follow directions pretty *gut*."

"You'll do just fine, Sarah. I just hope my arthritis don't make it too hard for me to keep my stitches even."

"*Mammi*, you don't have to make me a quilt. I could make my own when I have time."

"Child, I *want* to leave you something special. Something to remember me by. I shouldn't have talked about my old arthritis. It ain't gonna stop me—no way."

They spent the next hour talking about Deborah and her little ones. Martha told them how Deborah's husband, Ebenezer, had changed for the better, once Paul had talked to him.

"Paul is a *gut* talker, I guess," her *mammi* said. "Has he sweet-talked you yet?"

Martha blinked a couple times. She wasn't sure she wanted to pursue this line of questioning. She cocked her head to the side. "Not yet, *Mammi*, but we have some nice talks about the Revolutionary War."

Her grandmother began laughing till tears emerged from her eyes. "Well, that's a new one," she managed to say. "Talking war talk. Goodness, I guess I wouldn't call that sweet talk. *Nee*, not even close."

Martha had to smile herself. "Does talking about honeysuckle count as sweet talk? Because once when we were taking a walk together, we did talk about the wonderful smell from the honeysuckle vines."

Sarah grinned over. "That's a little closer, don't you think, *Mamm*?" she said turning to her mother who was wiping her eyes with a tissue as she controlled her laughter.

"*Jah, jah.* Next you'll tell me you talk about the martyrs," Sarah said.

"Oh dear."

"You do?" her grandmother asked. "Merciful day. It ain't like the old days. Your *dawdi* and I used to talk about flowers and birds and—"

"The bees?" Martha asked with a broad smile.

"Now, now."

"We'd better talk about something else, ladies," Sarah said. "We're getting off track now. Here come Melvin and *daed.* They'll be looking for a goodie. I hope we still have some of those cookies left."

"Not many, *Mamm. Daed's* been hitting them hard."

"*Jah,* he always does," Sarah said, shaking her head.

While they sat with the men, chatting amicably, they heard Lizzy's buggy coming down the drive. Melvin got up and went out to help her with the horse.

When she came in through the kitchen door, she held her arms out for her niece. "Look at you. You're a sight for sore eyes. We all missed you, Martha-girl."

Martha embraced her and kissed the side of her cheek. "I'm so glad to be home. I missed everyone, too."

"Well, we ain't gonna let you go off again, young lady. They'll have to find someone in Lewistown to help with the next *boppli.*"

Sarah went over to her sister and they hugged briefly and then Lizzy went over to her mother and leaned over to kiss her cheek.

"Any *kaffi* left? I was too lazy to brew a fresh pot. I saved enough for Leroy's afternoon break."

Martha went over to the stove and reached for the coffeepot. "I think we have enough for one more mugful."

Then she reached in the cabinet for her aunt's favorite mug—a red background with a black cat licking his paw.

When she set it in front of her aunt, Lizzy looked up and smiled. "You never forget, do you? *Danki.*"

"She knows what her *Aenti* Lizzy likes," Sarah said with a hint of jealousy in her tone.

Melvin walked back in and asked his wife when they'd be leaving. She looked over at her mother, questioning with her uplifted brows.

"Anytime you all are ready. I'm hungry, I don't know about the rest of you."

"I can always eat," Sarah answered.

"*Jah*, me, too," Martha added.

"Then let's get started," Lizzy said. "I hope they have burgers at the place you're taking us to, *Mamm.*"

When she told her daughter the name of the restaurant, she clapped her hands together. "They have the very best cheeseburgers around."

"And the best ice cream," her mother stated.

"I hope they have the raspberry and vanilla," Lizzy said as she walked out the door with Martha right behind her.

"Whose buggy should we take?" *Mammi* asked.

"Oh, let me drive," Martha said. "I didn't drive once while I was away. Paul always insisted on doing it."

"Paul?" Lizzy put her arm around Martha. "So, tell me you met a nice young man and you're madly in love."

Martha could feel her neck flush. Now why did she have to mention his name? "I wouldn't go that far, *Aenti*, but I did meet a very nice man, and we had a *gut* time together."

"They talked about the Revolution and the martyrs," her *mammi* said, grinning widely.

"Now ain't that nice," Lizzy said.

"You don't think it's weird?" Martha asked.

"Why would it be weird to talk about history. I think it shows a man with intelligence and an interest in something besides cows and corn," she stated.

Mammi shook her head, still grinning. "Did you and Leroy talk about wars and things?"

"Can't say that we did, but that was a long time ago, *Mamm*. I don't remember much about our courting days, except he was a mighty nice-looking *bu*."

"Like my Melvin," Sarah added. "He was the best-looking man in the community, and most polite, too."

"You know I remember him when he was a little guy. Of course, you were eight years younger than me and he was at least three years younger than I was. I didn't pay much attention to *buwe* that young."

"I'm glad we weren't in love with the same person, Lizzy. I remember Sally and Florence Schultz when they were young. They both went after the same young man."

"Who ended up with him?" Martha asked.

"An Englisher from town. Then he left the Amish. Never saw him again."

"Wow, *gut* thing one of them didn't marry him," Martha said.

"*Jah*, *Gott* had it all worked out, I'm sure of that," Lizzy said.

As they rode along the berm, Martha thought about God and Paul and she wondered what was in store for their relationship. Then she started visualizing the quilt to be made. Paul mentioned liking blue. Maybe blues would be nice for her new quilt. Different shades. *Jah*, *gut* idea. She smiled and encouraged Chessy, their driving horse, to pick up speed.

Chapter Seventeen

Lunch was enjoyable. Martha hadn't realized, until she was separated for a while, how much she loved her family. She wished Paul lived closer though, since it would be difficult to carry on a meaningful relationship being separated by a hundred miles.

As the women sat and enjoyed their ice cream after having burgers, Lizzy tried to get more information about Paul, but Martha avoided details. After all, it was way too soon to discuss a man she had just met.

Then the conversation went back to the quilt, and since it was a safer subject, Martha tried to keep their attention on that. "Will you let me work on it, too?" she asked, turning to her grandmother.

"I guess it wouldn't hurt, though it sure wouldn't be necessary."

"Maybe I'll work on placemats then. I like to weave."

"And you do a nice job, that's for sure," her mother said nodding. "Martha made me the nicest mats for my birthday."

"*Jah*, we've heard about that a hundred times," Lizzy said, rolling her eyes.

"I think you're just jealous that she never made any for you," Sarah said, glaring at her sister.

"But she embroidered two sets of pillowcases, don't you remember that? I bet those took even longer."

Martha had a pit in her stomach. She hated to hear such talk from two of her favorite people. "I just made what I thought each of you would enjoy the most," she offered.

Her grandmother clucked her tongue. "You two always get into these silly talks. Now stop it right now and finish your desserts."

The sisters turned to each other and laughed. "I guess we needed that," Lizzy said to Sarah, who nodded back.

"*Jah*, you sure did," their mother said sternly. "You're acting like little spoiled *kinner*."

Martha held back a grin. It sounded funny to hear two adults being reprimanded. It actually reminded her of dealing with the triplets.

After the bill was paid, they took the buggy to their favorite fabric shop and tethered the horse to a hitching post. There were so many colorful bolts of fabric to peruse, that they were there a good hour.

"How many different fabrics should I pick?" Martha asked her grandmother.

"Well, each star has eight points, but we only use two patterns per star. I'll probably make at least thirty squares and we want different stars…"

"I have some material left from curtains I made a few years back," Sarah said.

"What color, *Mamm*?" Martha asked her mother.

"They're the curtains in the small bedroom."

"Oh, they're blue and yellow flowers, right?"

"*Jah.*"

"That would be perfect!" Martha said. "That's a great start. Now I'll work off that."

Martha grabbed three bolts she'd been admiring earlier and laid them on a long table. "What do you think?"

The other women took their time deciding, feeling the cotton fabrics and weighing their decisions. Finally, Lizzy nodded. "I think they'd go *gut* together. Pick some more. I think it would be nicer to use three patterns in each star," she added.

"*Nee.* Way too much," Sarah remarked.

Before things got heated, Martha spoke quickly. "I'll have a few with three and the rest with two fabrics. That way everyone will be happy."

"You're the one who has to be happy," her grandmother said, frowning at her daughters once again.

"Well, I think that would make me happy," Martha said. "*Jah*, let me pick out some more fabrics."

The sisters avoided each other's eyes and went over to the stacks and picked out a couple they liked. Martha brought them over to the long table and made sure she'd pick out at least one of each of their suggestions—to keep everyone satisfied. This had turned out to be more of a project than she had imagined.

Eventually, the decisions were made and she had selected over twelve different patterns. Her grandmother told the saleswoman how much she needed of each fabric and while the woman was cutting away, Martha picked out a solid blue for her next frock. She pictured herself in the dress with matching apron, walking through golden fields of wheat with Paul. The color of the fabric, she was sure matched the color of his eyes. It was the color of the Caribbean, at least from the pictures she'd seen in magazines when she waited at the doctor's office.

Mammi complained her feet were hurting, so they headed back to the buggy and Martha took the reins after everyone was settled in and began the trek home. In spite of the occasions when her mother and aunt had their little tiffs, it had been a most enjoyable afternoon.

When they pulled up to the farm, there was a familiar buggy parked by the barn. Daniel Beiler had returned.

Paul was working on a maple dresser, which had been commissioned by the same family who had just had the kitchen cabinets installed. They had ordered a whole bedroom suite for their elder daughter's room.

His boss, Jeremiah, was working beside him on the bedstead. "You're real quiet today," he said to Paul.

"*Jah*. Not much to say."

"Mmm. Is it about that *maed* you brought by the day you picked up your pay?"

"I'd forgotten about that. *Jah*, I'm afraid it is. I miss her now that she's gone back home."

"It ain't real far. Why don't you visit her over the weekend?"

"Just like that?"

"Why not? What's the big deal? So it will cost you a little to pay a driver, unless you find a bus that goes that way."

"A driver is better. He'll take you right to the house and you can decide about the time. Maybe I will, but I don't know how to get in touch with her. Since it's Thursday already, I don't have time to write. Besides, I just wrote to her."

"I'd go anyway. If she ain't home, you can talk to her parents and try to make a hit with them. Never hurts to have a *gut* thing going with the family."

"You're right. *Jah*, I'll stop by Skip Davis's on the way home and see if he can drive me."

The bell went off, which rang when a customer entered the display room. "I'll get it," Paul said. "I'm done with this drawer front anyway."

He smoothed down his hair as he went through the swinging doors and stopped short when he saw Hazel, Deborah's sister, standing with a paper bag in her hands.

"Hazel! What brings you here?"

She cleared her throat and gave him a hesitant smile. "I made extra macaroons last night and remembered you saying how much you like them, so…"

"That's nice of you. *Danki*." He went toward her as she held the bag out to him.

"I wrapped them in foil to keep them fresh. I hope you like them."

"I'm sure I will." He took them and stood back wondering how to get back to work without offending her.

"I guess you're still working."

"*Jah*, lots to do, I'm afraid."

"Well, I won't hold you up. I haven't seen you since Martha left, and I just wondered how you were doing, now that she's gone."

"Fine. Fine."

"Are you planning on seeing her again, like soon?"

"No plans yet."

She smiled and let out a breath. "Well, I'd better get back to help Deborah, since I have to get home early. *Mamm* isn't feeling real *gut*, so I need to help out more. *Daed* still likes his supper prepared on time."

"It was nice of you to bring these by. *Danki*, again."

She still seemed hesitant to leave, but Paul felt there was nothing more to be said, so he started walking toward the swinging doors. By the time he reached them, he heard the front door open and then close. Without looking back, he went in to the work room and reached for the pieces to the second drawer. Jeremiah looked up.

"Customer?"

"*Nee*, a friend. She made macaroons. Want one?"

"Sure, why not?"

Paul opened the bag and pulled out a paper plate wrapped in foil, which he removed before passing the plate over to his boss.

"They look *gut*. Another admirer?"

"Just a friend."

Jeremiah put two in his mouth at once, closed his eyes and chewed slowly, allowing the taste to remain in his mouth. "She's a *gut* cook, I'd say."

Paul took one and ate it, then nodded in agreement. "*Jah*. Well, she does kind of like me, I guess. You know we dated before."

"Oh, Hazel, right? She used to stop by a lot. I remember. Sorry it didn't work out. Who broke it off?"

"I guess I did. I really liked the *maed*, but I wasn't in love with her."

"What about Martha? Do you think you love her?"

"If not love, I sure do like her a lot. We have a *gut* time when we're together."

"Maybe you'll know more after the weekend. Don't chicken out."

Paul grinned. "*Nee*, I won't. Here have some more," he said as he handed the plate back over to Jeremiah.

"Can I take a couple home to my *mamm*?"

"Help yourself. There are at least two dozen left. In fact, just leave me two or three and take the rest home."

"You sure?"

"*Jah*, I am. I don't want *gut* macaroons to sway my thoughts."

"Yup, you're a chicken, for sure," his friend said with a wink.

On the way home, Paul stopped at the Davis's home. Skip was cutting his lawn, but he stopped when he saw the buggy pull in. Saturday worked for him and they decided to start the trip around nine. That way he'd get there in time to take Martha out for lunch. Hopefully, she wouldn't have already made plans.

He decided not to stop off at Eb's place. He preferred not sharing his plans at the moment with his friends. He sure didn't want to be teased.

Chapter Eighteen

Martha felt her heart rate quicken as she reached for the screen door to the kitchen. She could see Daniel at the table with her father. They were drinking lemonade and finishing up the cookies Sarah had made.

Daniel nodded over at Martha as he continued conversing with Melvin.

Sarah came in behind Martha and again, Daniel barely acknowledged their arrival. Martha and her mother exchanged glances and then they went down the hall to the sitting room where they'd be out of hearing.

"I wish he wouldn't come by," Martha said, trying to control her emotions.

"He can be a strange one," Sarah whispered.

"Maybe now you know why I don't want to even consider him for marriage. I just wish *Daed* wouldn't encourage him."

"I'll speak to him about it. I sure don't want him for a son-in-law if he acts rude. I'm not comfortable around his family either."

"Thank goodness, at least you understand. While I'm

at it, I'd like to invite Paul to visit us some weekend. Do you think *Daed* would approve?"

"Oh dear, now that's another matter. Let's go slowly on that one, Martha. One thing at a time."

"*Jah*, okay." Her heart fell. She missed Paul much more than she had thought she would. Maybe more now that she'd had that episode with Daniel. She hadn't written to Paul about it, but if she saw him in person, she'd probably end up telling him.

"I'm going to go up and rest a few minutes. That way I'll be out of the way," Sarah said.

"I think I'll do the same. I'm suddenly way too tired to join the men. Besides, they barely looked up when we came in. So rude!"

"Your *daed* looked embarrassed. Did you notice?"

"I was too busy trying to avoid Daniel, *Mamm*. I'm so annoyed that he came back—even when I told him not to show up."

"You did? What on earth happened to make you so upset with him?"

"It's a long story. I'll tell you another time. Right now, I think I'll go write a letter to Deborah."

"*Jah*, you do that and rest a little. Maybe the young man will take the hint and return to his home. To his stimulating family."

Martha giggled. "I never heard you talk like that, *Mamm*. It's so unlike you."

"Oh, I feel guilty now. My *mudder* would wash my mouth out with soap if she heard me."

"I promise not to tell her," Martha said as she put her arms around her mother and gave her a hug.

Then they went upstairs, each to their own room to escape the men.

* * *

A few minutes later, while she was writing her letter, she heard her father come up the stairs. She had left the door open and when she looked up her dad was standing in the doorway with his hands on his waist, along with a major scowl on his face. "Why did you and your *mamm* leave the kitchen so quick-like? That seemed pretty impolite."

"We were tired, *Daed*, and neither of you said much to us. In fact, please don't be offended—but we thought you two were rude."

"Well, I don't appreciate you talking like that to me, young lady, but if I look through your eyes, I guess it did look like we were kinda ignoring you. Anyway, Daniel just left, but he gave me this note for you." He reached in his shirt pocket and handed her a small sealed envelope with her name printed on the front. "I have to go milk the cows now. Hope you have enough energy to make my supper soon."

"*Jah*, of course, *Daed*. Sorry if I sounded fresh. I really didn't mean to, but you need to know, I'm not interested in Daniel at all."

"I think you're making a big mistake, Martha. He's a Godly Amishman and would make a *gut* husband."

"Maybe for someone, but just not for me. I can't even stand to look at him anymore."

"Well, that's a shock. You were pretty smitten with him before you went away, if I remember right. I even asked a couple friends to plant extra celery, just in case."

"You can tell them to give it to someone else for their wedding dinner."

"Did you fall for someone else at the Lapp's? Is that what's going on?"

Martha could never lie to her parents and this was not the time to start. "I did meet a nice Amishman while I was there, but there's been no commitment on either side. I think he likes me, but we never talked about marrying."

"You sound disappointed. Are you in love with this man?"

"I wouldn't say that, but I really enjoy being with him."

"Is he proper with you?"

"*Jah, Daed.* Very. I was going to talk to you about him. I'd like to invite him here for a weekend so you can meet him."

"*Nee.* You can't be falling in love and marrying a man so far away from your *mudder.* It would kill her."

"*Daed,* we're only a couple hours apart. It's not like we'd never see you again. Besides, we may not even like each other, when we get to know each other better."

"Then there's no point in his coming. If you don't think you could marry the Beiler boy, then start attending the Singings again and find another beau."

"There's no one I'm interested in around here."

"You're being too fussy, Martha. I think you need to open your mind to Daniel Beiler again or start seeing more of the other eligible young men in our community. You may think the distance isn't that far, but we sure couldn't do all those roads with our buggy. It would be too dangerous, and your *mamm* is counting the days till she's a *grossmammi.* You know how she loves *boppli.*"

"I wish you'd at least meet Paul. I'd like your opinion. Maybe if it got serious, I could talk to him about moving to this area. He's a really *gut* carpenter and perhaps he could get a job with Stephen Shultz or one of the other carpenters around here."

He shook his head. "I'll think it over, Martha. Now let me go out and tend to the cows. Those ladies will be hurtin' if I don't get out there."

Well, at least his "no" didn't sound final. She'd have to work on softening his heart, and it might take a while for him to see it her way, but the thought of hurting her parents? She simply couldn't do that. No, Paul would have to move to the area or she'd definitely have to put him out of her mind and life.

She went downstairs and started heating the water for noodles for the chicken soup her mother had made earlier. She made sure there was plenty of fresh rye bread cut up, and then she decided to make a tossed salad to go with it. It was important to make her father happy. Real happy.

Then she remembered the note Daniel had left. Perhaps now he realized it wasn't going to work out for them and was breaking it off. She took the letter from her pocket and read it.

Dear Martha,
I know you were pretty mad at me the other day, so I came by to say I was sorry for what I did. I should not have done that. I hope you can forgive me.

I really care a lot and I think I love you. I think you loved me before you went away and I think you were real mad about me taking a girl home from the sing. But you should know I don't care about her the way I do about you.

I want you to give me another chance. I will

*try to be more happy around you. I guess I am
just used to my family and they are wonderful but
pretty serious a lot of the time.*

*I will see you soon.
Daniel*

Well at least he apologized. She had to give him credit
for that. He must have written the note before he came
over, so maybe now he was mad at her for not coming
down to talk to him. It was probably rude, but after all,
he barely looked her way when she came in.

Perhaps, once she got over her annoyance with him,
she could like him again. There was a time when she really thought she could marry him, but she couldn't blame
Paul for her change of heart, since she had been pretty
sure things were over when she left for Deborah's. Why
was life so complicated? In a way, it probably would have
been better if she had never met Paul.

A few minutes later, Sarah came down and reached
for her kitchen apron. When Martha explained everything was under control, her mother went out to work in
the vegetable garden instead of working with Martha.

The weeds were plentiful from the rains they'd received the past two nights and the pleasant cool breeze
of this early September eve encouraged her mother to
attempt the clean-up.

Before Martha added the noodles, she went up to
the mailbox where she found two letters addressed to
her—both from Paul. She nearly skipped back to the
house where she opened them immediately. While they
were full of news and light jokes, there was nothing
said about his coming, or wishing she would pay them

a visit soon. Disappointed, she tucked them in her apron pocket and went to the sink to wash her hands before shredding the lettuce.

Chapter Nineteen

Paul's mother asked him where he was going as he came into the kitchen carrying a bloated duffel bag. He began poking around the cupboards for something edible to take with him.

"I know you're going away, but you haven't said where."

"I'm just going to Paradise. I'll be home tomorrow."

"Where will you stay tonight? At that *maed*'s house? The one with the dark hair and eyes? What was her name again?"

"Martha. Martha Troyer. I've told you a couple times already."

"Hush your mouth, Paul. Sometimes I forget—especially names. Are you smitten with her?"

"And you've asked me that—at least half a dozen times."

"And your answer?"

"It's not changing. I like her very much. That's all I have to say."

"Mmm. Well, it costs money to travel by driver. Hope it's worth it."

"*Mamm*, please don't press it. You and *Daed* liked her, so there shouldn't be a problem even if it does get serious someday."

"*Jah. Jah.* So take some biscuits for the trip. They're fresh."

"*Danki, Mamm*," he said as he put his arm around her and kissed her cheek. "Sorry I've been grouchy. You're the best."

"Oh, now you're happy, but don't make me proud with your talk. It ain't fitting for a *gut* Amish woman."

"But you are the best. I know telling you the truth will not make you *grossfeelich*."

"I sure hope not. I don't like it when someone is all conceited like. What time should we expect you tomorrow? Will you be back for supper?"

"I'm not sure yet. Probably I'll be back by six or so, but go ahead without me."

"I'll save you some supper then. Say *hallo* to Martha for me."

"*Jah*, I will."

About ten minutes later, Skip Davis honked just outside the house. Paul went out the front door, waved to his father, who was exiting the barn, placed his satchel in the back seat and then climbed into the passenger seat next to Skip. The driver set his GPS, and they took off for the two-hour trip. Paul could hardly wait to see Martha's face when he arrived. What a great time to own a camera.

Martha was collecting eggs from the hen house when she heard a buggy come around the back of the farmhouse. She glanced up to see Daniel wave over to her as he pulled into a shady area and secured the horse's reins around the hitching post. She put the wicker basket over her forearm and stood waiting for him to approach her.

He nodded and gave her a hearty grin, more cheerful than his customary smile, which always looked slightly strained. "Hi, Martha. Get many eggs?"

"The usual, between three to four dozen."

"You must eat a lot of scrambled eggs."

"We give a lot of them away to family and friends, but we enjoy eggs for breakfast ourselves."

"*Jah*, me, too. I like them soft-boiled. *Dippy ecks.*"

"Mmm."

He reached for the basket and she handed it over. Then they began walking toward the house. "Did you read my note?"

"*Jah.*"

"Well?"

"Well, I'm glad you apologized."

"And you forgive me?"

"My faith gives me little choice. I must forgive."

"Do you mean it in your heart?"

"I'm not sure."

"But you'll give me another chance?"

"Daniel, I really don't think it's going to work out for us. I—"

"Please, Martha. I know I probably don't deserve it, but you're everything I could ask for in a *fraa*. I really think we'd be *gut* together. At least let me come by once in a while so we can talk and give things a chance to work out."

"I guess."

He reached for her hand with his free one, but she moved it quickly to her apron pocket. He seemed to get the hint, since he didn't attempt it again. He stayed around in the kitchen for about an hour while she put a salad together. Then he mentioned taking her to his farm to see the new buckskin quarter horse they'd just purchased. "We needed a new driving horse. Beautiful color. It shouldn't take long, and I can bring you back when you're ready."

Since Martha loved horses, and there was still time before dinner, she decided to take him up on his offer. She suggested leaving right away, before her father would be looking for his meal. This way she'd have an excellent excuse to return home quickly.

He pulled his buggy over and stopped for her to get in. He just sat in the driver's seat waiting, which annoyed her. She really liked it when a young man helped her into the buggy, though she could manage quite well on her own, *thank you anyway*.

As they headed toward the road, a green Chevrolet sedan turned onto the drive and headed slowly in their direction. Probably a lost tourist needing directions, she thought. Then the car stopped and who should get out but Paul Yoder!

"Oh, my goodness," she exclaimed.

"Know the guy?" Daniel asked, his voice low and sounding rather disagreeable.

"*Jah*. Stop, Daniel, I have to get out. We can go see the horse another time."

"*Nee*, you can see your friend *another* time. You promised."

"Don't be ridiculous! Let me out."

Reluctantly he pulled on the reins, but she jumped out of the buggy before the horse came to a full stop. Her landing was hard and her ankle twisted on the uneven ground. She cried out and went down on her knees in pain. Before she knew what had happened, she felt herself being swept up in Paul's arms. She heard Daniel calling out angrily for Paul to put her down, but he totally ignored the demand and headed toward the house.

"I hope you didn't break your ankle," he said to her with obvious concern. She looked into his tender eyes and knew at that moment that what she felt for him was more than friendship. A whole lot more.

She no longer heard Daniel's voice, but she did hear his horse trot at a quick pace over the gravel—more rapid than normal. Thank goodness, he was leaving without more dissention. Hopefully, he wouldn't come back. There was no point in it. She was very sure of that now.

"I can't believe you're here," she said. "Oh, Paul, it hurts real bad."

"My poor Martha." He managed to pull the screen door open in the front while holding her securely in his arms.

Sarah met them in the hall. The shock of seeing this stranger holding her daughter was almost too much. "You…you must be Paul?"

"*Jah.* That's me. I just got here, but I'm afraid your *dochder* may have broken her ankle."

"Oh, merciful day. Come, lay her on the sofa, please. She must be heavy."

"*Nee,* not a bit." He gently laid her on the three-cushion sofa and then Sarah reached for a small decorative pillow from the corner of the sofa and placed it under her daughter's head.

"I'll go get ice. Oh my, it's already swelling up."

While she was gone, Paul removed her leather shoe. He didn't touch her stockings, of course, and he made sure her skirt was covering her legs. Her modesty would be protected, that was for sure.

"I shouldn't have startled you by coming like I did. I didn't mean to spoil your date," he added, questioning with his eyes.

Her mother returned with ice wrapped in a plastic bag and a thin terry towel. "Here, let's see if the swelling goes down. Do you think we should take her to the doctor?" she asked Paul as he reached for the bag of ice.

"When the swelling goes down a little and she's in less pain, we can see if she can move it. It may just be a sprain."

"I don't think it's broken," Martha said. "It hurts terrible, but I didn't hear a cracking or a funny noise. Once when I was little, I was with a friend who broke his leg and you could hear it. Remember *Mamm*?"

"I do remember you telling me about it, but I wasn't there. I wonder if you should take an aspirin for the pain."

"I'd better not take anything. Just in case I need anesthesia."

"Oh dear Lord in heaven, I sure hope you won't," Sarah said, her eyes tearing up.

Paul looked over at Martha's mother. "I'm sorry I surprised everyone. I wish we had phones sometimes."

"It's okay. We don't normally mind company. We have lots of empty rooms. It's just better not to be surprised, is all."

Martha's mouth contorted. "Oh, that feels so cold. Can I take it off for a while?" she asked Paul and her mother. They looked at each other and her mother patted her daughter's shoulder. "I think you should try to keep it on longer, Martha. It's barely been on one minute."

"Maybe we can add a thicker towel," Paul suggested. "It does feel really cold."

"I'll go get a different one then."

After she left, he leaned over and touched her cheek. "I really missed you."

"And I, you," she said, smiling as much as she could through the pain.

"I couldn't stay away any longer."

"I got two of your letters at once. *Danki*. Did you get mine?"

"I did. They were so much fun to read. You have a *gut* sense of humor."

"You really think so?"

"*Jah*, I do. You make me laugh."

"We do have fun when we're together. I want you to know, that was Daniel you saw, but I don't really like him. I was just going to see their new horse, but I wasn't going to stay long. He comes over a lot, but I've told him it's over between us."

"And he won't take a hint?"

"*Nee*. It's way more than a hint, but he's so persistent, it actually scares me a little."

Paul's smile disappeared and his forehead furrowed. "I can go talk to him before I leave tomorrow and set things straight, if you want me to."

"Oh, that might get ugly. He has a temper."

"So do I, if I'm provoked. I won't fight, but I can make things clear."

"How do you convince someone when they know you can't do much about it?"

"Well, I've never had to do something like this, but I'm sure and certain, I'd think of something." His smile returned and so did Sarah with a thicker towel. She changed it and noted the swelling looked like it was going down slightly.

"Oh dear, I forgot I have a pork roast in the oven. It should have come out twenty minutes ago. Let me go take care of it. If you don't mind, Paul, you can stay with Martha in case she needs something."

"Mind?" He grinned. "No, ma'am. I sure don't mind. I promise to take *gut* care of her."

"I believe you will," Sarah said, returning his smile.

He knelt next to the sofa and took one of her hands in his and caressed it tenderly. She closed her eyes and tried to concentrate on his gentle touch, though the pain had only decreased slightly. To think he was right here next to her. What a wonderful surprise. She was so foolish to leap out the way she did. It was childish. Certainly, she could have waited the extra minute and emerged grace-fully. Oh, if she could live it over.

"What are you thinking, Martha? Was it a mistake for me to come without getting your family's permission first?"

"Oh no. I think it's better this way. They are too kind to make you leave." She smiled up at him. His face was close to hers and she could picture him kissing her, but of course, he wouldn't take a chance on her mother catch-ing them.

"How does your ankle feel? Any better at all?"

"I think it's a tiny bit better. It's going to be boring for you now that I have to sit around. I'm not even feel-ing *gut* enough to take a buggy ride. Maybe tomorrow I will."

"Martha, just being with you—seeing you is enough for me. It's been hard to concentrate. Fortunately, sand-ing doesn't take much thought and I've been doing a lot of that lately."

"What are you making now?"

He told her about the bedroom suite and went into some detail.

Sarah returned with a glass of water for Martha and then her father joined them. "My poor *maed*. Look at you."

He turned then to Paul. "I guess the shock of seeing someone uninvited was too much for my *dochder*."

"I'm really sorry I didn't ask about coming first."

"*Jah*, it might have helped."

Martha could tell her father was trying to contain his anger, but his words were embarrassing for everyone.

"Melvin, it will be fine. Paul is only staying the one night."

"Mmm. That's *gut*," he said pointedly.

"He's the nice man I told you about, *Daed*. Paul Yoder, this is my *daed*."

Paul rose and extended his hand. "*Hallo*, Mr. Troyer. It's nice to meet you."

There was a slight hesitation before Melvin reached over and shook Paul's hand—one shake—the Amish way. They dropped hands quickly and Paul asked if he could use their bathroom. Sarah pointed the way. "Up the stairs to the left. First door on the right."

"*Danki*."

After he was out of the room, her father spoke to her. "Well, young lady, did you know he was coming and just didn't bother to tell us?"

"*Nee*. Really, *Daed*. I was as surprised as you were."

Sarah nodded. "That's one reason she got hurt. Right, Martha? Did you fall from surprise?"

It was kind of a two-edged sword. If she said yes, her father might blame Paul. If she said no, he might think it was because she knew ahead of time.

"Maybe," she said, hoping to avoid either scenario.

"Now Melvin, you have to be more polite. He is our guest, whether you're happy about it or not."

He grunted and then patted Martha's shoulder. "Hope you feel better soon. Sprains can be mighty sore."

"I know, *Daed*." Her eyes began to shed tears. "Please don't be upset with me or Paul. He's such a nice person. Please say you'll give him a chance."

"I guess I don't have much choice. Now I need to get back to Millie. She's having more problems."

"I hope she'll be okay," Sarah said to her husband. "I'd feel real bad if she has to be put down. She's been a sweet cow all these years."

"We ain't there yet. I'll call the vet if she's not better soon though. I'm doing all the tricks I know."

As her father went out to the kitchen, they heard Paul's footsteps on the stairs. He had smoothed his gorgeous blonde curls back off his face exposing his smooth clear skin. He looked so handsome. Martha couldn't believe he cared so much for her—a plain and simple *maed*.

"Are you hungry?" Sarah asked Paul.

"I can always eat, Ma'am."

"I'm hungry, too, *Mamm*, but I don't want to walk yet."

"*Nee*, I wouldn't allow it. I'll bring two trays for you both, if that's okay."

"Perfect, *Mamm*."

"Maybe you'll need to help her eat," Sarah said, turning to Paul.

"I'd be happy to. Sure." He looked down at Martha with a huge grin.

"I'll feel like a *boppli*," she said.

"Let me get your trays," her mother said. "I made mashed potatoes to go with the pork, Paul. Hope you like them."

"That's one of my favorite meals. *Danki*."

Martha moved her foot. "Look, it's moving okay. I'm sure it's not broken."

"*Jah*, look at that. Does it hurt more when you move it?" Paul asked.

"It does, but not like before. The ice is getting to me again though. Can I leave it off a while?"

"Sure." He removed it carefully from her ankle and set it aside. A couple minutes later, Sarah came in carrying one of the trays. Paul stood and took it from her, setting it down on the coffee table in front of the sofa, which had been moved back a couple of feet after Martha had been positioned on the sofa.

"I'll come get the other tray for you," he said to Sarah, who smiled widely at his thoughtfulness.

When he returned with the second tray, he laid it next to Martha's. "Would you like me to start the blessing over the food?" he asked.

"Please." She closed her eyes and waited until she heard him rearrange the plates on the tray.

"This looks *wunderbaar*!" he said. "I'll cut your meat for you." After taking care of that, he asked what she'd like to eat first.

"I'd like the mashed potatoes, I think."

He placed a paper napkin under her chin and arranged a small amount of potato on a spoon and slipped it into her open mouth. After swallowing, she rolled her eyes. "I feel like a little kid. This is so embarrassing," she added.

"You'd probably do the same for me."

"Of course."

He placed a second spoonful of potato in her mouth and grinned. "I bet you were an adorable *kinner*. It's a shame there are no pictures to prove it."

She nodded as she swallowed. "Are you sorry I'm not a blonde like you?"

"Sorry? Goodness, I love your beautiful eyes and the color of your hair. I just wish I could see it let down. Is it very long?"

"To my waist."

"A couple nights ago, I tried to picture you with it all loose around your shoulders."

"Why?"

"I don't know. Maybe because someday I hope to really get a chance to see it."

"Only my husband will," she said cryptically.

"I know." He caressed her hand and then offered her a piece of meat.

"Your dinner will be cold, Paul. Why don't you stop and eat some of yours?"

"I'll take care of you first."

"I'm not hungry anymore. In fact, my stomach is a little queasy. Maybe because of the fall."

"I'm sorry to hear that. All right. I'll stop for a while." He cut his own meat and then ate his meal. "Your *mamm* makes *gut* pork, for sure."

"*Jah*, she cooks everything really great. I watch her a lot, hoping some of it will rub off on me."

"I have a feeling it will. Your *mudder* seems nice,

Martha. I just hope your *daed* will give me a chance to prove myself."

"Prove yourself? In what way?"

"That I'd be okay to be part of the family."

"Paul, are we going too fast? Sometimes I'm afraid of what I feel."

"I know what you mean. I've never had such strong feelings for a *maed* before. I think *Gott* may have brought you to the Lapp's in order to bring us together."

"I'm just afraid being apart most of the time, you may change your feelings about me."

He shook his head. "It sure hasn't happened yet. You're all I think about."

She wiped a tear from one of her eyes.

"Martha, did I say something wrong?" He put his fork down and knelt next to her. "Why the tears?"

"I'm not sure. I guess I never expected someone to care this much for me. A guy anyway."

"Obviously, that Daniel guy feels this way."

"*Nee*. I don't think he's capable of such deep feelings. That's one reason I would never marry him."

"I thought you were engaged at one point."

"He never actually proposed. Thank *Gott* he didn't. I might have said yes in a weak moment."

"I think I should go talk to him tomorrow. I don't want him hanging around you."

"I don't think he will. Will you come back to visit again soon?"

"It depends on your parents, Martha."

"Maybe I'll take a nap soon and you can go talk to my *daed* about…things. Nothing about us. But it would be *gut* for him to get to know you better. I think *Mamm* already likes you."

That perked him up. "Really? She's a real nice lady. You can tell her, I like her, too."

"I will when I have a chance. I really can't eat anymore, Paul. Can you eat mine as well as your own?"

"*Jah*, that's for sure. It's delicious and I didn't eat much this morning. Too nervous, I guess." After finishing both plates of dinner, he looked over. Martha's eyes were closed and he realized she had fallen asleep. Perhaps now would be a good time to improve his relationship with her father. He quietly took the two trays to the kitchen and then took a deep breath and headed out to the barn.

Chapter Twenty

Deborah checked the clock. It was only eleven in the morning, but she was exhausted already. She'd hoped her sister, Hazel, would have come by earlier to lend a hand. At least the boys were playing outside with her husband working nearby. He'd certainly been better since Paul Yoder had spoken to him about helping, though sometimes she feared he didn't keep a close eye on the boys, especially now that there was the harvesting. It was a busy time, for sure.

The twins were fussing in their cribs, but she'd nursed them and they seemed satisfied when she first laid them down. Hopefully, they'd settle down soon and take a nap.

Deborah took one of Martha's letters she'd received the day before and re-read it. Not a word about Paul. Perhaps she'd imagined her friend's interest in the handsome young Amishman, who was such an important part of their circle of friends and family. She wondered why he hadn't been by today. Usually on Saturday, he came by to help with the animals. Perhaps he needed to work for his boss. Apparently, business was booming. It would be so nice if he and Martha married and lived nearby. She'd become close to the lovely dark-haired Amish girl, who was so good with the children. Oh, how she wished she were still there to help. Things seemed much smoother when she was in charge.

Deborah looked around at the kitchen. Dishes had accumulated in the sink and the floor felt sticky underfoot again. Maybe she and Hazel could tackle the cleaning again. There just didn't seem to be enough hours in the day—or energy in her body.

Eb had listened to her the night before when she suggested they sleep separately for a few months. She made it sound like she just wanted him to get more sleep. In reality, she feared he would become amorous and things would happen between them. She sure wasn't ready to get in the family way again. She wondered if she ever would.

Maybe Martha would come back in a couple weeks to help again. The next time she had time to write to her, she'd ask if it would be possible. She knew Martha was very attached to her parents and might not want to leave them again. Certainly, that would be a problem if she and Paul got serious about each other. Deborah was pretty sure Martha would not move away from her family, and Paul was doing well in his carpentry field and was even checking out homes in the area. Knowing Hazel still had an interest in Paul, it would probably make more sense for him to consider her. *Jah*, she'd mention it next time she saw Paul.

When Martha woke up, she looked over at Paul, who was reading a copy of the weekly Amish newspaper, *Die Botschaft*. What a wonderful picture of a contented man.

"Hi," she said softly.

Immediately, he laid the paper aside and went over and knelt by her side. "You had a nice nap. Feeling any better?"

"I think so. See if the swelling has gone down at all."

He moved a quilt her mother had laid over her while she slept and lightly touched the sore ankle. "I think it does look a little better. How does it feel?"

"Well, I need to go upstairs, so I'll soon find out."

"Let me help you." He went over as she moved her legs over the side and sat for a moment waiting for her slight faintness to subside.

"I'll try to walk on it."

"I don't think you should. Not yet."

"I think I can make it."

He put one arm around her waist and told her to lean against him. She rather enjoyed that, though the pain radiated up her leg. "Oooo, it hurts bad still."

"I'm going to carry you then." He was about to lift her in his arms when she stopped him.

"Please ask my *mudder* to come up, too. I need to… well, you know."

"Oh, right." He called out to Sarah and she came into the room quickly.

"Goodness, should you be walking already?" she asked her daughter.

"I have to go up, *Mamm*. I may need your help."

"I can carry her up, since it hurt too much for her to walk on it," Paul said.

"*Jah, gut.* I'll follow behind. I think you need to put her down by the bathroom. Right, Martha?"

Martha's neck turned scarlet as she nodded. How embarrassing!

Once he had her near the bathroom, he set her down

gently and moved away for her mother to take over. "I'll wait by the stairs," he said.

"*Gut*," Sarah said and helped her daughter into the bathroom.

"I'm so embarrassed," Martha whispered.

"It'a just a normal function. I'm sure your Paul occasionally has to go, too."

"It's just…well, you know."

Once she was done and washed her hands, she was able to make it to the hallway.

"Maybe you should stay up in your room till you're able to do the stairs by yourself," her mother suggested.

"But then I won't see Paul."

"He could stay in your room with you for a while. I trust you."

"That means a lot to me, *Mamm. Danki.*"

Instead of being carried, Paul merely supported her as she walked to her room. She sat on the side of her bed while he went down to get the ice pack. Her mother propped up some pillows before helping her lie back, and then she covered her legs with the quilt from the bed.

Paul returned and her mother tucked the ice pack around her daughter's ankle, covered it up again and left the two alone.

"You must be so bored," Martha said to Paul.

"Not at all. I just like being with you. Do you want me to read anything to you?"

"Well, I didn't do my Bible reading this morning."

"*Jah*, come to think of it, I didn't either. I'm reading through John for the umpteenth time."

"Oh my, so am I! What chapter are you on?"

"The tenth."

"And I'm on the eighth! That's such a coincidence."

"Maybe not a coincidence," he said, smiling over. "I'll start with the eighth then." Her Bible was on a table next to the bed, so he pulled a chair over, reached for the book and began reading. His voice was deep and resonated in the small room, even though he spoke softly. She closed her eyes and listened to the Word. When he read verse 12, she asked him to repeat it.

"When Jesus spoke again to the people, he said, 'I am the light of the world. Whoever follows me will never walk in darkness, but will have the light of life.'"

"I love that verse. I think of that sometimes when things are going wrong in my life. I try to keep my eyes on Jesus and it really helps."

"*Jah*, it does. I read the gospels often."

"So do I, and John is my favorite."

He reached over and took her free hand in his. "You look so lovely when you talk about *Gott*. Your eyes light up."

"He's the light of life! Just like it says."

"I want to see you often, Martha. If your parents are set against my coming here, would you visit me in Lewistown—at the Lapp's? I'd be happy to pay for the driver."

"I do have a little money saved. I wouldn't want you to pay for it."

"I'm making a nice income. I'd really want to help out."

"I think my parents will be okay in time. *Mamm* is already. Did you have a chance to talk to my *daed*?"

"I went out, but he was in the fields working, so I didn't think it proper for me to distract him. Besides, I wanted to be near you, in case you needed something."

"You're so considerate. I'm sure my ankle isn't broken. It's beginning to feel better. I think I'll take an aspirin now. Would you check with my mother for me after we're done reading the Bible?"

"Of course. When you're feeling well enough, maybe we can go for a buggy ride and you can show me all around the area. When I'm back home, I want to picture you in the places familiar to you."

"I think with aspirin in my body, I'll be well enough soon to take that ride."

They heard voices from downstairs and Martha recognized one male voice. "I can't believe it! Daniel is back. He'll never give up."

Paul replaced the Bible back on her table and headed for the door. "I'll go have a nice talk with him."

"Paul, be careful. Please don't get involved."

"I am involved. You said you feared him, and that's not *gut*."

When he got downstairs, Daniel was standing in the hallway talking to Sarah. He looked up as Paul came into view. "What are you doing here? Were you in Martha's room?"

"It's not any of your business."

"*Excuse me, stranger.* It's very much my business. Martha's going to be my wife—"

"Not according to her."

"She's just fooling around with you. Can't you tell when a woman is mocking?"

"Now please, Daniel, Paul," Sarah began, her lower lip trembling. "I'll have to ask you both to leave if you're going to act like this. My *dochder* is not committed to either one of you."

"You know better, Mrs. Troyer," Daniel said, turning to her, his voice loud.

"Don't speak to Martha's *mudder* like that," Paul said. "That's disrespectful."

"I came by to talk to Martha, not you," Daniel stated as he pushed past Paul to reach the staircase. "I'll go take care of her. You'd better not be here when I come down."

"Look here, I don't want to argue with you, but according to Martha, she's tried to make it clear to you that any feelings she had in the past, are gone."

"I want to hear it come from her lips, not a creep like you."

Paul's hands curled into fists and it took everything he had to keep from using them. "You're not going to go up and be alone with her."

"I don't want anyone up there with her," Sarah said, practically in tears. "I'm going to go get Mr. Troyer. He's not going to be happy about any of this."

Paul turned around and climbed two steps and took hold of Daniel's shirt. "You heard her. Get down here. We'll settle this outside."

"*Jah*, we will. I hope you don't bleed easy."

"Oh dear," Sarah mumbled as she ran towards the back door to get her husband.

Martha stood at the top of the stairs, leaning against the railing. "What's going on? I heard arguing. Why are you here, Daniel? I've told you not to come by."

"I was worried about you. I came to make sure you're okay."

"I am. I'm getting better. Please leave now. Don't cause a scene."

"It's your friend here causing a scene. I'm not about to let a complete stranger tell me what to do. You and I are going to be man and wife someday. I have a right to protect you from men like him."

"Daniel! Get it straight! I'm never going to marry you! Now, leave!"

Paul put his hand on Daniel's shoulder. "Leave on your own, or I'll make you leave."

"Oh really, big guy? And you're going to make me?" He let out a frightening laugh—the same kind she'd heard the night he forced a kiss on her. It sent shivers up her spine.

Without releasing his hold, Paul shoved him down the hallway and out the door, though Daniel resisted with all his might. Martha made her way down the stairs, one at a time, but they were already on the front lawn by the time she got to the foot of the stairs.

It had gone from a war of words to a physical battle. She watched in horror as they took turns being the aggressor. Blood was pouring out of Paul's nose, but Daniel had a definite limp as he rose from the ground to attack once more. All of a sudden, Melvin came running around the corner of the house with Sarah right behind him. Melvin got between the men somehow and pushed them so hard, they both found themselves on the ground, stunned by the older man's strength.

"I want you both out of here and don't either of you show up here again—ever. My *dochder* is not going to have anything to do with either of you! Got it?"

Daniel got up first and picked up his straw hat, which had laid several yards away. He smoothed back his hair, placed his hat on top of his head, and made his way to his buggy, still shuffling one leg. He didn't speak a word. He slapped his horse with the reins and took off without turning his head. Sarah thought she heard him speak under his breath. She believed he said he'd be back. She prayed she was wrong.

Paul stood up and Sarah handed him several tissues for his nose. By now the front of his shirt was crimson. His crushed hat lay off to the side. He leaned over and picked it up from the ground and tried to reshape the rim. Then he looked directly at Melvin. "I'm sorry, sir. Truly. I didn't want it to get to this point, but that man is dangerous. I wouldn't let him see her again."

"I don't intend to, nor do I intend to let you come back and take advantage of my *dochder*. She's a fine young woman and deserves better than the two of you. You'll have to leave now. You'll find a phone about a mile up the road at a service station."

"May I say good-bye to Martha?"

Melvin shook his head. "*Nee*, and don't bother to write. I'll see to it that she don't get the mail before me, so don't waste your time."

Sarah lowered her head. She didn't want Paul to see her tears.

"I'll leave then, but can I at least have my satchel back?"

"I'll get it and put it out front. Then the doors are gonna be locked. If I have to, I'll get in touch with the head bishop and he can call the police."

"That won't be necessary, sir. I'll leave without a fuss." Paul looked over at the front porch. He could see Martha behind the screen door, leaning in pain, with tears streaming down her face. What had he done? How did everything turn so ugly so fast? He held up his hand and then threw her a kiss, which she returned. Then she turned away and disappeared from his sight.

Martha made her way up the stairs, pulling herself by the rail to take weight off her ankle. It was a nightmare. Only an hour before, she'd been so happy. She could still hear Paul's deep voice as he read from the Bible. She'd felt sure his being there was a gift from God himself. Now this. Her father would be keeping an eye on her every minute. He'd always been over-protective, but now…

She laid back down on the bed and looked over at the empty rocker. She could barely make it out through her tears, which seemed inexhaustible. Then she felt her mother's touch.

"Are you okay, dear?"

"*Nee*. I'll never be okay again, *Mamm*," she sputtered out through her tears.

"Oh, sure you will. Somewhere there is a nice Amish—"

"I don't want to hear it. I want Paul. I know he loves me and I love him. Everything is Daniel's fault."

"Now it takes two people to have a fight."

"But he pushed it. You don't know what Daniel did to me."

Sarah drew back. "What did he do? Tell me right now."

"He forced a kiss on me. It was so rough and horrible. I hate him."

"Hush now, don't say that. You know *Gott* doesn't allow us to hate."

"How can I help it? I don't want to, but he's ruined my life. Oh, I want to be with Paul. *Daed* was so mean to him."

"You know Amish people don't fight, Martha. It's totally unacceptable."

"But it was all Daniel's fault. All of it! Paul was just defending himself, and me."

"I'm so sorry, Martha. I know it's difficult right now, but soon you'll forget all about that young man. It will just be an ugly memory."

"My memory of Paul will never be ugly. He was so kind to me—always."

"You didn't really know him that well now, did you?"

"We saw a lot of each other when I was helping Deborah. We talked by the hour. I do know him well, and I love the man he is."

"Martha, you'll have to make an effort to forget him. Your *daed* will never approve of you seeing him again. You know that. Please, don't make things worse."

"I don't want to hurt you—either of you, but I'm a grown woman now. I need to follow my heart."

"You're still in our home, under our protection, you must do as you're told. It doesn't matter how old you are. That's the way it is."

"Then I'll leave."

"Martha, please…don't say that. You'd break my heart. My darling girl, you're the light in my life."

"*Nee Mamm. Gott* is the light in your life."

Sarah sat back and stared at her daughter. "*Jah*, He's first, but you're flesh and blood. It's a special love. Someday you'll understand."

Sarah remained for nearly an hour, caressing her daughter's hand and cheek until Martha finally fell asleep from exhaustion and pain—and the need to escape the reality of her life.

Chapter Twenty-One

Martha laid on the sofa the next day. She couldn't concentrate enough to read, which normally would help pass the time. Her parents and grandparents had left for church, leaving fruit, a glass of milk, and a blueberry muffin on the table next to her. At first her mother had wanted to remain home with her, but she convinced her that she'd be fine. She could do the stairs now, taking them slowly, one step at a time, so there was no reason for nursing care.

She no longer used the ice and the swelling had gone down significantly. Before they left, her mother appeared concerned, but her father still seemed angry. He said very little to her, and she avoided eye contact with him when they were in the room together.

The tears continued off and on. The pain in her heart made her wonder if she'd ever know happiness again. When she thought she'd never see Paul again, she'd burst into a new round of weeping. Martha hoped Paul's driver had been able to come right back for him so he wouldn't have to spend the money for a motel room.

Paul was probably even attending his church service

right now, which he hated to miss. Maybe he was even sitting where he could see Hazel, who most likely was wearing her newest frock to attract his attention.

Perhaps it was better this way, since she wouldn't have to move and disappoint her parents, and he could stay at the carpenter's shop and be near his own family.

Finally, she ate part of a banana and laid back on her pillows, which her mother had brought down from her bedroom.

She heard a faint knock on the front door. Who would be here on Sunday? Perhaps it was a robber, checking out the house. She limped to the window in the front and peeked out at the caller. *Oh, glorious day!* It was Paul! In spite of her pain, she nearly ran to the door and flung it open. "I can't believe it's you! I thought you went home."

He stood grinning with his hat in hand. "Is it safe to come in? I was hiding out by the workshop till I saw your parents leave for church service and I waited a few more minutes in case they forgot something and came back. I hope you're not upset with me."

"Paul—how could I be upset? Come in quickly."

He closed the door behind him and took her in his arms. She never wanted him to let go. They stood like that for several moments before he asked her about her ankle.

"Much better now. Look." She lifted her skirt slightly to show how the swelling had receded. "Where did you stay last night? I thought you'd be able to catch your driver before he got too far."

"I didn't try. I couldn't just leave like that, knowing how upset you were. I actually stayed in your barn. I walked a long time first, but once it got dark out, I figured the safest place would be on your property. At least

I hoped your *daed* wouldn't discover me and call in the police. I knew they'd probably go off to church."

"I'd better sit. My ankle is throbbing a little." He followed her to the sofa and after they sat, he put his arm around her and drew her close again. This time his lips searched hers and they remained entwined, his lips traveling to her cheeks and her forehead.

"My *lieb*," he kept whispering. "I love you so much. I can't let you go."

"Paul, I feel the same way. I realize now how much I love you."

"We have to marry, Martha. We can't let them separate us."

"It would kill my *mudder*. I want so much for them to see you for who you are and love you, too. Maybe in time..."

"We have no time. They won't even allow us to see each other. We can't live like this."

"I think they'll change over time."

"How? I'm not even allowed to visit you?"

"Oh, Paul, I don't know what to say. There's nothing I want more than to be your wife, but all my life I've wanted to do it the right way. A special moment—with all my friends and family around us. *Gott* would want it that way. We have to make my parents change."

"I'm afraid to leave you here."

"Because of Daniel?"

"*Jah*. The man is crazy. I never struck a person in my life, but he looked like he wanted to kill me. He might come back and do something to you, Martha. I can't let that happen."

"I am afraid of him—more now, than ever. Maybe I'll go back and stay with Deborah. That way I can be near you and away from Daniel. Then slowly, my parents will come around. I know they will."

"You know them far better than I do, Martha. If you think they would one day accept me, I'd be willing to wait. Especially if I knew you were nearby and safe. We can't wait forever to marry though. My feelings are so strong, as it is. It will be hard to keep apart from you, you know what I mean."

She nodded and looked down at her hands. "*Jah*."

"Will your parents even consider you staying with Deborah again, knowing I live nearby?"

"I don't know. Maybe if Deborah writes to them and says she really needs me. Her last letter made it sound like things were getting difficult again, so it probably would be true."

"We can try, but what if it doesn't work? Then would you be willing to run away and marry me?"

She nodded slowly. "I think I would. My dear *mudder* is the only problem. I know how much it would hurt her—never to see me again? Goodness, I don't know if I could do that to her. Remember, I'm her only child."

Paul placed his head in his hands, elbows on his knees. "If only I hadn't let him get to me."

"Who struck the first blow, Paul?"

"Daniel, of course. I could never have hit him first."

"Then you were acting in self-defense."

"The Amish don't look at it that way. You know that. Don't forget the martyrs."

"I'm afraid you're right. Four years ago one of the members was shunned for punching a man, even though he hadn't started it. I hope *Daed* doesn't go to the head bishop about all this. He may, though. My *dawdi* is a deacon. He might have some influence. I just don't know."

"How long does your service last? I'll have to leave before they come back."

"Oh, Paul, when will I see you again? I'm not even allowed to get your mail."

"If you're not allowed to come to Lewistown, I'll find a way to come back here. I don't like to be sneaky, but we have to see each other. I've decided to buy you a cell phone and one for myself. I'm not sure how to use them and you'd have to find a way to recharge it, but that way we could at least talk to each other and make plans."

"If my *daed* ever found out…"

"You'd have to keep the sound off and just check it from time to time. We'll work something out. We have to." He removed her *kapp* and ran his hand over her bun. "Someday you'll let your hair down for me. Someday we'll be man and wife. We have to keep that in our minds or we won't get through this. Even if we have to leave the Amish."

Fresh tears escaped her eyes and she shook her head over and over. "I can't leave the Amish. I simply can't. We have to work it out so we'll remain Amish. Please agree."

"I'd get on my knees in front of the whole congregation and confess my sins for you. I'd do anything."

They stayed in each other's embrace for another hour, not even talking much, just enjoying the closeness. Occasionally, she'd turn her face to him and they'd kiss, sometimes too amorously, and she'd pull away slightly till they had better control.

"I never understood what it was to feel passion," she said once. "I think I know now. It's a little scary because I'm a single *maed*, but if we were married…"

"*Jah*, that makes all the difference. We'll remain apart until *Gott* blesses our union."

"Paul, you need to get more food. Let's go in the kitchen and I'll scramble you some eggs or something."

"I guess I'll take you up on it, but let me do the work. You can sit and boss me around."

She smiled and they walked hand-in-hand into the kitchen where he cooked them both a batch of eggs. They each had a muffin with leftover coffee.

"How will you get back to Lewistown?" she asked.

"My driver will return at five, as we originally scheduled. It may be tricky, because he was supposed to pick me up here, but I can wait up the road and stop him when I see the car."

"I'm going to ask my friend, Naomi, if you could send mail to her place and then I can stop by and pick it up."

"Would she do that?"

"I'm sure. We're very close. We'd do anything for each other. Before you leave, I'll write down the address for you."

"That's better than nothing, Martha. Do you see her often?"

"I'll make a point to. She's always home. She takes care of her baby *schwester* and her other siblings, so she doesn't get out much. In fact, she's talked about leaving the Amish, though I think it's all talk. She likes to grumble," she said with a grin.

After they ate, Martha washed the dishes. Paul dried them and she told him where they were stored. "I don't want to leave anything out that would show I had company," she said.

"I'm glad we're not like an English family I know, who had cameras every which way in their home."

"Why would they do that?"

"They have two *kinner* and I guess they want to know what they're doing every single minute."

"Goodness, that seems so strange."

"They're really into their technology. Their kids have all kinds of 'I' things. I pads, I phones, I pods! I don't even know what they all do."

"Sounds kind of silly. *Kinner* should be outside playing with their friends, not stuck inside, hiding away."

"It is strange, when you think of it. Martha, I think I should leave before your family comes back. I don't want more trouble for you."

She dried her hands and moved slowly over to him. He put his arms around her and they were silent for several minutes. Finally, he broke the quiet. "I'll write as soon as I get home and mail it to your friend. Maybe I'll have a chance to buy the phone for you. Do you think it would be all right to mail that too?"

"Wait until I talk to her. I wouldn't want her to get in trouble with her parents. They're ever so strict. I'll let you know if it would work out. I'll somehow get a letter off to you, too, Paul. I'll need to write it in secret. I hate this."

"*Jah*, I do, too, but it won't be forever. I promise."

They walked over to the front door and he kissed her lightly on her nose. "Don't forget, I love you, and someday we'll be together for *gut*. Don't get discouraged."

She fought back tears and smiled as broadly as she could. After he left, she stood following his every step as he moved further away from her. Finally, he was nearly out of her sight. Just before he made the turn, he stood motionless for a moment and then waved to her. She blew a kiss to him, closed the door, and wept, once again.

Chapter Twenty-Two

Later in the week, *Aenti* Lizzy came by to work on the quilt for her niece. Martha made no further offer to help. It made her too melancholy to be working on a bridal quilt, which might never be necessary. She tried to keep her spirits up, but her future looked bleak. She would either have to give up the man of her dreams, or her family, if she moved away with a man they didn't approve of. Reconciling with Daniel was totally out of the question. Though she didn't fear his returning to the farm, she did worry about seeing him again—even at the church meetings.

Perhaps that wouldn't even occur, because she had overheard her father speak about bringing Daniel's behavior before the Bishop, which could mean a *bann*, unless Daniel convinced everyone he regretted his outrageous behavior and was willing to humble himself before the congregation. She doubted he would be willing to ever admit being at fault. It would be wonderful if he was forced out of the community altogether and she would never have to set her eyes on him again.

Things were strained between Martha and her father.

He rarely spoke to her, unless it was absolutely necessary. Even her mother seemed somewhat remote.

When Lizzy arrived, Martha's mother and grandmother were waiting in the kitchen for her. They sat together for coffee before starting on the quilt and when Martha made an excuse to not join them, her aunt looked disturbed.

"We haven't chatted together for a while, Martha. You look upset. What's troubling you?"

Martha looked at her mother, who appeared distracted as she placed the mugs around the table.

"I'll be all right, *Aenti*. I'd rather not talk about it."

"Oh, problems with the opposite sex?"

"Lizzy, I don't like that expression used in front of my *dochder*."

"Oh goodness, Sarah. She's not a *kinner*."

"Even so."

Martha's grandmother laughed aloud. "My proper *dochder*. And don't say 'pregnant' around her, Lizzy. She don't know how that happens."

As the two older women laughed, Martha bit her tongue so she wouldn't join them. She looked over at her mother, who was fuming, but remained silent.

"I'm going to clean the shower upstairs, *Mamm*," Martha said as she went into the cleaning closet for the supplies.

"I thought you did that on Friday."

"Well, it needs cleaning again."

"You'll be the Proverbs 31 wife," her grandmother said, nodding.

"She'll never stay up all night," Lizzy said. "She sleeps seven hours a night. Ain't that right, Martha?"

"When I can."

"You don't look like you got any sleep last night," her *Mammi* said.

"I barely did."

"Then take a nap instead of cleaning," Lizzy suggested.

"I'll see. Maybe later." She went upstairs carrying a bucket with sponges and brushes as well as vinegar for cleaning. When she got to the bathroom, she glanced in the mirror over the sink. Dark circles under her eyes made her look ten years older. If Paul saw her now, he'd want to break off with her. She wondered how he was fairing. She'd already written over ten pages of her letter intended for him, which she had hidden in her dresser. She planned to add more before heading to her friend's house. She just hoped Naomi would be willing to play interference for her.

It would be so nice to have a cellphone, even if she only talked to Paul once a week. She missed his soft voice. She missed his caress and his gentle eyes. She just missed everything about him. Oh, if only Daniel hadn't come by, things would be so different. Wishing wouldn't help anything and she even questioned whether her frequent prayers would help. At least, they gave her comfort and a certain peace. She felt close to God and knew He loved her—even more than Paul. That in itself, was a blessing. It was a reminder to always put God first, and she needed reminding—frequently. Paul was never far from her thoughts.

After scrubbing down the entire bathroom, which was clean when she started, she took a sponge bath and changed into fresh clothes. Then she brushed out her long hair and plaited it, twisting the long braid to fit under her *kapp*. She might not be able to do away with the purple under her eyes, but she could at least look well-groomed.

By now her father had come in from the barn and they were about to eat their main meal.

Lizzy looked at her niece and grinned. "Now don't you look pretty?"

Her father glanced over with a frown. "*Jah*, she's a mite too pretty sometimes."

"Now what would you be meaning by that, Melvin?" Lizzy asked, placing her hands on her hips.

"Too many *buwe* find her attractive. Nothing but problems. Didn't you tell your *schwester* about the big fight?" he asked, turning to his wife.

"I didn't think it was necessary."

"Well, I sure want to hear about it. Who was fighting?" Lizzy's eyes lit up at the prospect of some gossip to share.

"You can tell her what happened," Martha said, suddenly losing her appetite. "I'm headed over to see Naomi. I haven't seen her since my trip."

"You're going to eat first, ain't you?" her father asked.

"I'm not hungry, *Daed*. I'll grab an apple on my way out."

"Now I want every detail, Sarah," Lizzy said. "Just let me help dish out the soup first."

Normally, Martha would kiss her *aenti* good-bye, but today, she was annoyed by the pleasure the woman seemed to be getting from what might be the hardest day of Martha's life. Even though she didn't know what had transpired, or how much it had affected her niece, there would be no hugs today.

After making her way in the buggy to Naomi's house, she secured the reins around their fence post and headed toward the kitchen door.

* * *

Naomi was sitting on the small porch, rocking her sister when she saw Martha come up the path. Her face changed from boredom to pleasure as she stood to greet her. "I'd heard you were back, but I've been too busy to stop over. I rarely get away from the house, but boy, have I missed you, Martha."

"I've missed you, too. I'm sorry I didn't get to write more, but I was really busy most of the time."

"I can't believe all you did. I hope it was appreciated."

"I think it was, and anyway, that's not why I did it. I like helping others, though that sounds like I'm bragging. I don't mean it that way."

"I know you don't. You're a *gut* person. Have you heard from Daniel? He hasn't been with Molly lately. Have you gotten back together?"

"No way. I have so much to tell you. Do you have time?"

"Let me put Patty down for her nap first."

"Goodness, she's getting big. Hi, sweetie," she said, turning her attention to the smiling baby.

"She's such a *gut boppli*. Better than my *bruder*, that's for sure."

"Where are they today?"

"My *mammi* has them at her place. She's teaching them to husk corn. '*Gut* luck,' I told her. 'They don't do anything I ask of them.'"

Martha giggled. "That's because you're their *schwester*."

"I guess so. I'll be right back."

Martha sat on a glider as Naomi's mother, Mrs. Shoemaker, came out and offered her some iced tea, which she accepted along with several oatmeal cookies. Her appetite had finally come back.

When the mother returned to see if she wanted more tea, she had two of her toddlers in tow, yanking on her apron. Goodness, it reminded Martha of being at the Lapps with all these little ones around.

The weather couldn't have been nicer. There was a slight breeze, which rustled through the oak trees surrounding the house, and the sky was a deep blue with wispy clouds racing across the horizon. She moved over to a rocker and creaked back and forth, humming to herself.

When Naomi returned, she was carrying a large wicker basket with damp clothes. "Keep me company while I get these hung."

Martha helped by handing her the clothespins as they moved along the line. "Perfect day for drying," she added.

"You mentioned a Paul Yoder in your letters, Martha. I had the feeling you were getting pretty fond of him."

"*Jah*, even more than that. We're in love!" It felt good to use those words—for the first time.

"Wow! That's great! Has he met your parents yet?"

The elation she'd felt, dropped to her feet as she proceeded to tell her friend everything that had transpired, leaving out no details. The wash had all been hung, but they continued to stand and talk about the ups and downs of Paul and Martha's relationship.

"You'd leave the Amish for him?" Naomi asked.

"I couldn't do that to my parents."

"But you're in love! You may never find a man like him again. You *have* to marry him!"

"It's true, isn't it? I'd be giving up so much to cut it off. Even for my dear *mamm*."

"She'd get over it, Martha. If he's as wonderful as you say he is, he could make her like him, whether she wanted to or not."

"But I don't know about *Daed*. He was the maddest I've ever seen him. The only *gut* thing that came out of that day, was Daniel being told to never show up again."

"Have you seen him at church? I've missed the last two services. I've had a miserable cold, but I'm finally getting better."

"I'm glad, Naomi. Colds are miserable. I didn't go to the services either, because of my ankle."

"You walk pretty *gut* now. I'm glad you didn't break it."

"*Jah*, me, too. It sure hurt a lot though. It was a stupid thing for me to do. I felt so embarrassed after it happened."

"How did it feel to be carried by a guy?"

"Well, because it was Paul, it was wonderful."

"Is he cute?"

"*Jah*, handsome. Really, really handsome."

"Oh, you're so lucky. I still don't have anyone interested in me. It's getting harder and harder to stay here. *Mamm*'s expecting again, you know. I'll never be free."

"Well, don't go running away. You'd be sorry if you did that."

"If I had a place to go, I'd be gone. With all my sitting experience, I could get a nanny's job in an instant."

"Naomi, listen to yourself. Why would you leave here to go do the same thing for strangers?"

"But they'd pay me and maybe I'd go back to school

and learn computers or something. I'm just not cut out for this life."

"You'll change your mind when you find the right man."

"If…I find the right man. Does your Paul have any single *bruder*?"

"*Nee*, he's the youngest. All the others in his family are married."

"Oh well, I tried. I'll never meet anyone as long as I have to take care of *Mamm*'s brood."

"You know you love them."

"That's not the point. I need my own life."

"That's where I have a problem. I feel that way, and yet I can't imagine leaving my parents. Mainly my *Mamm*. I love her so much. She counts on me for everything."

"She made out okay while you were away, didn't she? She even has her mother still living. She'd survive, Martha. You need to think of yourself, just for once."

Martha mulled that over in her mind and let out a sigh. "I'll think about it. In the meantime, here's my letter to Paul. Did the mail truck come by yet?"

"Not till later. I'll walk you up to the box and you can flag it."

Naomi placed the empty laundry basket on the porch just as her mother opened the door, holding her two-year-old son. "Here, take him and change him, Naomi. I need to feed the others. They're fussing up a storm."

Without a word, Naomi took the squirming toddler from her mother's arms and carried him to the mailbox as well. "See what I mean?"

"You sure do stay busy."

* * *

By the time Martha reached home, it was time to help with supper. Eat, clean, cook. That was an Amish woman's life, but in her mind, it had rewards of its own and she did not consider it a burden. Not as long as that life was shared with a mate you cherish.

Chapter Twenty-Three

A few nights later, following their supper and scripture reading, Melvin set his Bible aside. "I'd like to tell you both what's going on, so you don't hear about it from someone else." He cleared his throat and shuffled about on his chair.

Martha and her mother exchanged looks. It was unlike Martha's father to discuss important matters in the evening. If anything was on his mind to deliberate, it was usually brought up at the noon meal, before grace was even said.

"I've talked to Bishop Josiah about Daniel Beiler and he's going over to the Beiler's place tonight. That young man is in serious trouble, and he's not going to get away with it. We can't have physical attacks on people and still call ourselves Amish. I don't know if the bishop will want to talk to you two about it. I merely told him everything I knew; but you were there from the beginning. Since the Yoder boy ain't a member of our district, there's not much we can do about him, though the bishop might write an account to that young man's district."

"But he didn't start it," Martha said.

"I didn't ask for your opinion, Martha. It don't matter who started what, they both used their fists—a terrible thing."

Martha's heart skipped a beat. She immediately prayed against news of this incident going any further. It could ruin Paul's reputation if it got out, and he'd probably lose his job as well as his standing in his community.

And it all started because of her falling and hurting her ankle. If only Paul had gotten word to her about coming, she would not have been in the buggy with Daniel to begin with. So many "ifs" to consider. She had to accept what actually happened and do the best she could to get through it without becoming bitter or angry.

"What would happen if Daniel doesn't accept blame for his actions?" Martha asked.

"Most likely, he'd be banned. He's a trouble maker, I'm afraid to admit. I didn't see that side in him before, but he should have let you get out of the buggy right away, and just gone on home, nice and polite-like."

"*Jah, Daed*, exactly, and he shouldn't have been at our place to begin with. I had tried to end it with him more than once. He didn't respect my feelings."

"He forced a kiss on our *dochder*," Sarah added, her jaw clenched.

"Is that true?" Melvin asked Martha.

She was sorry it was brought up, but since it had, she nodded.

"Is that all he did to you?"

"That's bad enough, don't you think?" Sarah asked him.

"*Jah*, it's bad, but I feared something worse."

"And if he had done…something…much worse, *Daed*, what would you have done about it?"

He pulled on his beard and looked into space before answering. "I would have prayed for strength to forgive and the ability to get through it without violence; but if the state had come in on it, I would have let justice be served."

Sarah shut her eyes and shook her head. "Mercy, how do people get through some things."

"I hope Daniel does get banned and has to leave. I don't look forward to seeing him after this. I don't trust him. Maybe I should go stay with Deborah until this is all worked out."

Melvin's eyes seared into hers. "So you could be near that Paul fellow, right?"

"Well, that's not what I meant."

"I wasn't born yesterday, girl. I know exactly what you meant."

"Dad, she wrote to me asking for help. I can even show you the letter."

"She'll have to get help elsewhere. You're not going anywhere. Let that be the final word on the subject."

Martha knew better than to argue with her father. He was loving and kind, but he was also a stubborn, strict Amishman and one did not pursue a discussion he put a stop to. She learned that early in life. Her mother was somehow different. She would usually bend in any direction for her daughter, but this time she remained silent, as well.

"I hope I don't have to talk to the bishop about it," Martha said, twisting her apron strings around her fingers. "I wish you hadn't told him."

"I had no choice, Martha. It's not something I enjoyed doing. Daniel wasn't at the church service Sunday. I'm sure he's pretty ashamed of himself."

"And well he should be," Sarah added.

"When will you see Bishop Josiah again, *Daed*?"

"He plans to stop by tomorrow sometime. You'd better be ready for him to question you about it, Martha. Maybe you should write it all down before you forget what happened."

"I'll never forget any of it. That was the worst day of my life."

Her parents both stared at her. "Are you serious?" her mother asked.

"*Jah*. Dead serious. I'll never see Paul again and…" She couldn't go any further. She placed her head in her hands and began to weep.

"Now merciful me, all this fussing over a man you hardly knew," her mother stated, shaking her head in disbelief.

"You just don't understand. He loves me, too. We even talked about…marrying…" she managed to say through her tears.

"Well, I'll be," Melvin said raising his hands in disbelief. "It's a shame you have to get this upset, Martha. We had no idea it had gotten that far in your head."

"Oh, *Daed*, could you give him a chance? I know if you got to know him, you'd like him a whole lot. He's kind and he makes beautiful furniture and he's *gut* to his parents and to me and—"

"Now, that's enough for one evening. I will pray about this whole thing. I need a little guidance from upstairs, Martha."

"Oh *danki*, *Daed*," Martha said rushing to her father's side. She knelt by the chair and put her arms around his waist. She'd never shown this much affection to her father in her whole life, and he was as close to flabbergasted as an Amishman can get. He was actually speechless.

Sarah put her hand to her mouth and let out a German phrase which Martha couldn't even translate.

"Now let's get ourselves together and I'll read more from the *gut* book. Maybe a nice quiet Psalm would settle us all down," her father said, his voice shaking.

"*Jah*, Melvin. *Gut* idea."

Martha resumed her position on the sofa next to her mother, who reached across and grabbed her hand while Melvin began reading Psalm 89. At first, Martha concentrated on every word, and then she found her mind wandering to Paul. When would they see each other again? Everything seemed so hopeless, though there was a crack in her father's resolve; she felt it. Perhaps in time he would relent. Oh, that he would. *Dear Gott, please…*

Paul found it difficult to concentrate as well. He was glad most of the work for the next three days would be routine and not require much thinking.

He never should have allowed his anger to take over. He could have taken the blows and remained calm with a little more effort. If Martha hadn't expressed fear, and if he hadn't seen with his own eyes the ugly hatred and rage in that man's eyes…well, he could have had more control and this whole nightmare wouldn't be taking place. Thank goodness he had stayed overnight in the barn Saturday so he could spend time with her the next day while her family was attending church.

She had looked so forlorn as she stood staring through the screen door on Saturday, he knew he couldn't leave without being with her once more. Sunday, they declared their love and that knowledge would have to keep them from feeling hopeless, at least until they could be to-gether permanently.

Today he planned to purchase cell phones. They didn't have to be fancy and expensive like he'd seen English people carry. He certainly didn't need, or want, the Internet. The devil worked overtime harming young people with his lies. No, he had no desire for the temp-tations he knew existed in the cyber world. It was hard enough staying pure in his world, which was narrow in-deed and confined to those of similar beliefs.

"Paul, did you hear what I said?"

"Sorry, I wasn't listening real *gut*."

"We have to go price out another job later. A man stopped by before you came in this morning. He wants a shed built for his tools. We'll close up here a little early."

"*Gut*. I have errands to run when we're done, as well."

"You sure don't seem happy since you visited your *maed*. Do you want to talk about it yet?"

"Maybe later. It's too hard to talk and work at the same time."

"It went kinda bad then?"

"It couldn't have gone worse."

"There are other fish in the sea."

"Not for me. And it's not that she doesn't care for me. Oh well, I may as well give you the whole story." He stopped what he was doing and laid the sandpaper aside.

Jeremiah did the same and motioned over to their desk where two wooden chairs stood side by side. "I need a break anyway. *Kaffi*?"

"*Nee*. I've had too much already."

Jeremiah poured himself a mugful from the pot and they sat together. Paul started from the beginning and went through the whole encounter, remembering every detail as if it had just happened. When he talked about leaving Martha behind on Sunday and the pain he felt, he nearly lost it.

"No wonder you're upset. I hope our bishop doesn't get wind of it. You'd be in a lot of trouble."

"I hadn't even considered that. Well, I've got enough on my mind without adding that possibility on top of it. Thanks for listening, Jeremiah. It did help to talk about it. I haven't said a word to anyone else. *Mamm* keeps asking me how things went. I just wish she'd stop."

"*Mudders* do that. I'm asked at least once a day why I'm not married. If it's not my *mamm*, it's one of my *schwesters* or a friend. Maybe I don't want to get married. Did they ever think of that?"

"Don't you?"

"Well sure, but I haven't found a *maed* I'd want to live the rest of my life with. I'm only twenty-five—the same age as you. Hopefully, someday I will."

The day dragged on, and finally they closed the store and went to the man's home, which was on the other side of Lewistown, to give an estimate for the shed. Then they parted company and Paul purchased the phones at a local shop. He went home and took a paper bag from his mother's stash and cut it up for wrapping paper, adding Naomi Shoemaker's name and address. At least they had someone willing to help with their subterfuge. They both hated living with lies, but they could see no other way. The one thing they could not do, was break up their relationship, so what choice was there?

He shook his head and hid the package under his bed

until the next day when he planned to stop at the post office to mail it. The sooner, the better. His heart was as heavy as a tractor, that was for sure.

Chapter Twenty-Four

It was visiting Sunday and instead of going with her parents and grandparents to visit relatives in the next town, Martha took the open buggy over to Naomi Shoemaker's home. She had tucked a five-page letter she'd written for Paul in her apron pocket before leaving the house. Hopefully, there would be mail waiting for her at Naomi's.

Once they were alone in her friend's bedroom, Naomi retrieved a small package along with three letters from the bottom dresser drawer. "I can't wait to see what's in the box," she said as she watched Martha tear at the wrapping paper. Inside was a note and a small cell phone, along with a recharge wire and instructions.

"Oh, my goodness," Naomi said softly. "I can't believe it. You could get in real trouble if anyone finds out, Martha."

"No one will know besides you, dear friend, and I know you'll never tell."

"My lips are sealed. Was it from Paul?"

"*Jah*, he bought himself one, too. That way we can talk once in a while. I'll recharge it at the library when the battery is low. I have no idea how to use it, but I guess I can figure it out."

"Show me when you do. I'd love to call someone. Trouble is, I don't have anyone to call."

One of her brothers knocked on her door. "*Mamm* needs you, Naomi."

"Oh, all right. In a minute."

They stuck the phone back in the drawer along with the mail Martha had brought. "I'll have to mail this tomorrow. Just don't forget the phone before you leave," Naomi reminded her.

"Don't worry about that. I'm so excited. Maybe he'll call me tonight."

"It came two days ago."

"He's so sweet, Naomi. I can't wait for you to meet him."

"Me, too. I'd better go see what *Mamm* wants. I thought I'd get a little time off, but it doesn't look that way. She depends on me more every day, but I have some *gut* news. Her *schwester* from Ohio is coming to stay for a month or more and it will give me some time off. I'm actually hoping to go visit some relatives while I have the chance."

"Where do they live?"

"Not far. Only about an hour's drive, but it's far enough so that I won't be able to be my *mudder*'s slave for a while."

"The bishop came by to hear my side of the story about Daniel. He went to the Beiler's the night before."

"I wonder what happened," Naomi said.

"He wouldn't say. Everything is hush-hush. I think my *daed* knows, but the subject isn't allowed to come up. I just pray they don't get in touch with Paul's bishop and get him in trouble. He was just defending me, is all."

"*Jah*, but you know what the *Ordnung* says about violence. It sure makes it plain we're not to lift a hand to anyone in anger. Though I've known homes where it's happened."

"*Jah*, and everyone keeps silent."

"It seems to be, if it's in self-defense..."

"*Jah*, but then read the stories of the martyrs. They were amazing."

"Still."

"I know."

When they got down to the kitchen, Naomi's mother was stirring soup, holding the baby in her other hand, with two toddlers pulling on her skirt.

"It's about time. Here take Patty. She needs to be changed. I sure can't do everything."

"When's Cousin Esther coming?" Naomi asked as she took her sister from her mother's arm.

"Tomorrow, thank the Lord."

"You know I'm planning on going to visit Valerie after she gets here."

"You've told me enough times. *Jah*, I guess we'll manage a few days without you."

"It's part of my *Rumspringa*, *Mamm*. It's my right."

"You'd better not jump the fence, Naomi."

"Patty sure needs a change," Naomi said, quickly changing the subject. "Come up with me, Martha. Isn't she ready for her nap?" she asked her mother as she turned towards the hallway.

"You can try. She's awful fussy today. Getting another tooth, I think."

"I'll rock her first. Poor kid."

After cleaning her up and rocking her for half an hour, the baby fell asleep in her arms. Naomi laid her down and the girls went back to her room where Martha retrieved her letters from Paul along with the package. She placed them in her pocket and the girls went out to the buggy.

"Where should Paul send the mail now?"

"I wrote down my cousin's address. Here," she said, pulling a small paper from her apron. "I don't know how long I'll stay, but now that you have a phone, you can call him after you hear from me. Your folks will think the mail is just me writing, I guess."

"I'll give you my phone number now so if you can get near a phone, you can call me," Martha said.

"The *gut* news is my cousin has a neighbor who's a Mennonite and she owns a phone, so I can call you. I can't wait."

"I think I could be a Mennonite, don't you?" Martha asked. "I'd love to have air conditioning."

"Your folks would have a fit if you left the Amish."

"I don't plan to switch, but I just thought I'd mention how I feel."

"*Jah*, maybe I could do the same. They believe in Jesus and all, but they have prettier clothes and some even have cars," Naomi mentioned.

"I know. What's so bad about that?"

"Nothing, as far as I'm concerned. You know they pray different from us, too. Like Jesus is a friend, kinda."

"So I've heard. Sounds a bit odd, don't you think? Anyway, *danki*, for all you do for me. We'll keep in touch."

She sang all the way home. Letters from Paul, yet unread, and a phone! Glory be, what a wonderful day!

* * *

Daniel's father paced up and down the long sitting room while his wife and son sat together on the navy sofa. His brothers and sisters were told to go to their rooms.

"How could you bring such shame to this family? What on earth was in your mind to strike another person?"

Daniel remained silent.

"I want to know! How could you let some *maed* affect you like that? There are plenty of girls."

"Not like her."

"You have to go before the congregation and get on your knees!"

"I don't think it was that sinful. He struck the first blow."

"It don't matter. You know better. You turn the other cheek. Besides, that girl told a different story."

"She was lying."

"You're done with that family. I never liked them to begin with. Always laughing and smiling like there wasn't anything upstairs in their brains. Nix in the head."

"I didn't like the family either," his mother stated, scowling. "Nothing but trouble and not plain enough."

"The bishop will be back to make arrangements for your confession."

"What if I don't think it was a sin?"

"Are you serious? You'll be banned! Excommunicated! Shunned! Is that what you want?"

Daniel shook his head as he looked down at the floor. "I hope they make that Paul guy get on his knees. He's even more bad."

"I told our bishop to find out who's in charge of his

community and he promised he'd get right on it. We have to keep the Amish faith pure, that's for sure."

"*Jah*," his wife said, nodding. "For certain. That girl should have to be punished as well, encouraging men to fight over her."

"I doubt that will happen," Daniel's father stated, his forehead creased. "You know her *dawdi* is a deacon."

"Can I go now?" Daniel asked.

"You can go do the milking—by yourself. And do some soul searching while you're at it. Shameful!"

Daniel tiptoed out of the room, went to the barn, grabbed a huge bale of hay and threw it as far as he possibly could, nearly striking one of the cows. Then he shouted profanity, causing several of the cows to low in fear. He had no intention of humbling himself before the congregation. He'd rather go to Siberia! How could he have been fooled into thinking Martha was someone he'd want to spend his life with. The tramp! Playing one man against the other! His mother was right. There should be consequences for her, as well!

Chapter Twenty-Five

That night, Martha excused herself immediately following the family devotional time. Normally, she'd sit and work on the mending with her mother and grandmother, or read the newspaper, but she was hoping against hope that she'd received a call from Paul. After closing her bedroom door, she laid the phone on the bed and read through the instructions. Paul had already placed his phone number in the contacts. It was the only number. She held the phone to her ear after pressing it and waited. His voice came up and he said on a recording, "Please leave your name and number. Thank you."

She hesitated and then said, "It's me. You have my number." Then she hung up. Her heart was palpitating like the wings of a hummingbird as she sat waiting for a response. Within two minutes, she saw the phone light up and she grabbed it and pressed what she hoped was the right key. Sure enough, Paul's voice came across the air. "Martha, it's you."

"*Jah*, and it's you," she said and giggled into the strange instrument. "And you're far away."

"Oh, it's so *gut* to hear your voice. Talk to me more."

"I don't know what to say. *Hallo*."

He laughed. "When we're together, I can hardly get a word in edgewise."

"Oh, dear, am I such a *dummkopf*?"

"I'm teasing you, Martha. You're far from dumb. *Wie geht's*?"

"I guess things are fine, though I miss you with all my heart."

"My *lieb*."

"Do you miss me, Paul?"

"More than you'll ever know."

"I picked up the phone today at Naomi's, but she plans to be away for a while, so you'll have to mail letters to another address for a couple weeks or so."

"Do you know the address yet?"

"She gave it to me, but I'm not sure of the date she leaves. She was hoping for tomorrow, but it depends. I can call you when I know, right? Like I did? Am I *schmaert* to figure it out already?" she said rather proudly.

"*Jah*, you are smart."

"The bishop came by, Paul. He wanted to know about the fight. I tried to make it sound like you barely did anything. After all, Daniel struck the first blow."

"I'm so ashamed of how I acted, Martha. I wish I could live it over."

"But he pushed you into it."

"I'm an Amishman. I should have more control."

"I hope they bann Daniel. I never want to see him again."

"Was he at the church service?"

"It was visitation week, but he wasn't at the one last week. I asked Naomi."

"How is your ankle?"

"So much better. The swelling went down. You can hardly tell it ever happened."

"I'm so glad. I've been praying for you."

"*Danki*. I pray for you every day, too. How are we going to ever see each other again?"

"I'm hoping to come soon. We'll have to plan my visit for the weekend they have church service, so we can spend some time alone together. Right now though, we're in the midst of harvesting. My one brother has been sick, so it's been difficult. Especially when I've been putting in longer days at the carpentry shop. Orders are piling in."

"That's *gut*, no?"

"*Jah*, normally, but at harvest time…"

"True. It's been beautiful weather here, but I'm not looking forward to winter."

"Can you plan a trip somehow when things settle down? Maybe come back to see Deborah?"

"Oh, my *daed* wouldn't let me return. He made that more than clear. I wish he'd relent and let you visit us here. We have so many empty rooms."

"*Jah*, that would be the best solution, but I doubt that will ever happen. We may have to run off and marry, Martha. You know that."

"I can't do that. I simply can't break my *mudder*'s heart. I'm counting on my parents coming around to accepting you, Paul. That's my prayer. Please make it yours as well."

"I have prayed that same prayer, Martha, but knowing how strong you feel about it, I'll make it my strongest request as well. If we do things right, *Gott* will honor us."

"It has to work out for us, Paul. It has to."

"I can call you tomorrow night again, if we say good-bye now. We have to save our battery as much as possible.

Remember to keep it on vibrate. I'll only call in the evening, around this time, so you won't have to keep it on you. I don't want you to get into trouble. In fact, press the button on top and turn the whole phone off during the day."

"Okay. I hate to say good-bye."

"Then we won't. We'll just end by saying how much we love each other."

"*Jah*, I like that ever so much better."

After they confirmed their love, Martha hung up and held the phone on her lap for several moments before turning it off to save the battery. What a wonderful-*gut* gadget this little phone was. Surely, in time, the Amish bishops would soften towards them. Hopefully, in her lifetime.

She hid the phone and charger under her clean night clothes and closed the drawer softly. She heard her parents coming up the stairs. Perfect timing. Though she felt guilt, it was overcome by her love for Paul and the need to hear his voice and words confirming his love. Surely *Gott* had brought them together for a purpose.

The following day, Paul stopped by Eb's house to check on his friend. It was the first evening he got off work at a decent time. He was surprised to find Hazel and her older sister, Wanda, both at the house. Normally, they'd be home by now.

Hazel's eyes lit up when she saw Paul standing at the door. "We haven't seen you lately, Paul. You've been busy, I guess."

"Between the carpentry business and working on the harvest, I haven't had a chance to stop by. Where's Eb?"

"He just went upstairs to help with the *buwe*. Want some coconut cake? I made it today."

"Sure, that's one of my favorites." He sat down as Wanda came in from the next room where she was folding diapers. She greeted him and then went outside to check on the blankets she was airing on the clothes line.

"It's late to be doing the wash, ain't it?" Paul asked Hazel as she laid an enormous piece of cake before him.

"Deborah's been sick and she *kutzed* all over the bedding."

"A virus?"

She shook her head. "I don't think so."

"Bad food?"

"*Nee.* Not that either. I think…she thinks…she might be in the family way."

"Already?" He realized too late, he'd embarrassed Hazel by pushing her for an explanation. She was blushing.

"Well, that's nice, I guess," he stammered.

"I guess so. She sure has been feeling poorly. I may stay the night."

"You're a *gut schwester*, that's for sure."

"I try to be. Of course, I don't have my own family to worry about, so it's not hard for me to share my time. Maybe someday…"

"Oh, *jah*, that's for sure. Someday."

He cleared his throat and managed to place a large portion of cake on his fork. "Mmm. *Gut.*"

She grinned over. "*Jah*? I'll give you some to take home, if you'd like."

"Oh, that's okay. My *mamm* always has dessert lying around. I don't want to get too fat."

"Oh, you're not fat! You're perfect. Well, just about…" Her cheeks continued to glow red.

Eb came down and joined them. "Hi, stranger. Hey, any more of that cake left, Hazel?"

"Oh, *jah*, a lot. I'll cut you a piece."

He sat down across from Paul. "So how's it going? Heard from Martha?"

Paul glanced over at Hazel, who concentrated on cutting a large piece of cake for Eb and avoided looking over as the men discussed Martha.

"*Jah*," Paul answered.

"Bet she sure misses you."

"I guess so."

"When will you go see her again?"

Paul shrugged. "Can't say."

Hazel placed the plate in front of her brother-in-law and then excused herself to check on Deborah.

"Don't go into the *buwe*'s room," Eb called after her. "They're being punished for screaming and waking the twins."

"I'll just go check on my *schwester*."

"Did you hear we're expecting a *boppli* again?" Eb asked proudly.

"*Jah*. I thought you were going to wait awhile."

"That's hard to do, Paul. Someday you'll understand."

"It's just that Deborah has her hands full now..."

"But I help her more than I used to. Thanks to you, I figured with my help, we could handle another. Maybe it will only be one this time."

"I kinda hope so." Paul moved the empty plate over to the sink and sat down again.

"Tell me about Martha. Are they gonna let you stay with them soon?"

"It sure doesn't look that way."

"That's a shame. Guess you won't let your temper get you going next time."

"Don't remind me. I still feel so guilty about striking a man."

"I'm surprised you haven't heard from the bishop over it. You know how news travels."

"If they talk to me about it, I'm ready to take my punishment. It might help if I did kneel before the congregation and get it over with."

"The best thing would be if no one ever says a word about it. After all, most guys would have reacted the same way you did."

"English guys, maybe. Not *gut* Amishmen."

"I don't know what I would have done if it had been me. I hope I could hold back, but I don't really know."

"My nose still bleeds sometimes at night. I don't know what he did, but it looks crooked, don't you think?"

Eb leaned over and stared at his friend's face. "Turn sideways."

He did and then looked back at Eb. "Well?"

"I think it is a little crooked. Not too bad though, or I would have noticed it before. I bet it got broke."

"Serves me right, I guess."

"Didn't Martha say anything?"

"She'd be too sweet to tell me it looked bad."

"It ain't real bad, Paul. Just a little bit bad."

"You're a big help. Well, I think I'll head home. We're finally done with the harvesting."

"*Jah*, most of us are. It was a big yield this year. Perfect amount of sun and rain."

"It was. Heard we're headed for a hard winter, though. The almanac says at least two blizzards for this area."

"Sometimes they're wrong."

"But sometimes, they're right on. Well, we have to take what the Lord gives us."

Paul closed the door behind him since it was getting breezy. When Hazel returned, she went to the door and watched through the pane as his buggy moved down the lane to the road. How she wished she could stop caring for the man. Maybe God would send someone new to her. At night, when she was alone, she sometimes cried herself to sleep. Even though Martha and Paul didn't see much of each other, they had the comfort of knowing they loved each other. She should be happy for them. She really tried, but it just didn't happen. God forgive her.

Chapter Twenty-Six

Naomi tucked her hairbrush in the small suitcase next to her toothbrush. She'd packed three dresses, along with a sweater and underwear and a night gown. She didn't need much. At the last minute, she added extra stockings and a pair of sneakers. She was fortunate that her neighbor offered to drive her to her cousin's house and didn't even want payment. It was Mrs. Downing from across the street and she'd always taken a liking to Naomi and her family. In fact, she occasionally brought over a casserole or a bowl of pasta to help out. Once she even helped hang out sheets.

When she carried the suitcase down the stairs, one of her brothers, eleven-year-old Bruce, almost knocked her down by mistake. "You're not supposed to run! I'm telling *daed.*"

"Oops, but you didn't fall."

"I could have."

"So where are you going?"

"I told you, to cousin Valerie's."

"When are you coming back?"

"I don't know for sure. Not for a while, I hope."

"You just wanna get away from me."

"All of you! I'm plumb wore out."

He raced off to get something from the boy's bedroom. "Hope you stay forever," he shouted back.

She rolled her eyes and went down the stairs where she placed the suitcase by the front door. She could see her neighbor driving down their driveway, so she went into the kitchen and said good-bye to her mother and aunt, who was giving her baby sister a bottle of juice. She leaned over and kissed Patty's forehead.

"How will we get in touch with you?" her mother asked as she continued to knead the bread.

"I'll find a phone somehow and call Mrs. Downing."

"I hope it won't be long. You know how miserable I feel some days."

"*Jah*, I know. I just need a break."

She turned and went to the front door. Mrs. Downing waved through the car window and Naomi saw the trunk flip open all by itself. So cool. She placed her suitcase inside and closed it manually and then climbed in the front passenger side. They had a nice trip and Naomi couldn't take her eyes off the passing landscape. The autumn colors were ablaze. When she was driving her buggy, she was too busy watching traffic to really enjoy the view, so she thoroughly enjoyed being a passenger.

Once she arrived at Valerie's clapboard house, she thanked her neighbor and went to the front door and knocked. Valerie, who was the same age as Naomi, grabbed her and hugged her profusely. "I can't believe you're here! We're going to have a ball!"

Naomi giggled and hugged her back. Valerie knew lots of people—many of them Englishers. This was going to be a trip to remember.

* * *

Every evening around half past six, Martha found an excuse to go to her room, where she turned on her phone and waited for Paul's call. He was almost always on time and they tried to limit their calls to ten or fifteen minutes. So far, she still had enough of a charge. When she heard about Deborah being sick, she asked if he knew why. When he hesitated, she let out a moan. "Oh no, not already. That's just too much."

"Eb thinks because he helps out a little now, that they can manage a classful of *kinner*, I guess."

"Now she really will need me. I wonder if my parents will let me help out."

"That would be *gut*. Then we could see each other every day. Try to convince them. It's sure no lie that she's gonna need all the help she can get. Her *mamm* rarely comes by. I guess she's busy with her other *kinner* having *boppli*."

"I'll work on *Daed*. Have you heard anything from your bishop?"

"*Nee*. Not a word. I don't think he's heard from anyone about it."

"Do you feel less guilty?"

"*Jah*, I pray for forgiveness every night."

"You're such a *gut* man, Paul. Try not to take it too hard."

"*Danki*, my sweetheart. We'd better go now. Tomorrow night?"

"*Jah*. Same time. So far, no one has wondered why I disappear at the same time every evening."

After they hung up, she replaced the phone and went downstairs. Her mother looked up. "We were just going to play a game of Scrabble. Want to join us?"

Martha smiled over at her mother and grandmother. "I'd love to. Are *daed* and *dawdi* going to join us?"

"*Nee*, they're in the sitting room talking about the farm and the weather and all. That's what makes them happy."

While they spread the game out on the kitchen table, her *mammi* asked about her disappearance every evening.

"Oh, I just like to have a few minutes alone, is all."

"You seem better about things," her *mammi* said. "You're getting over your feelings for that boy from Lewistown?"

Her mother looked up as Martha stammered. "I… I'm not really over anything. I still care a whole lot."

"Well, at least you're not clambering to go back to Deborah's," her grandmother added.

"She'd go in a heartbeat, if we let her," Sarah said.

"I think she's in the family way again," Martha said as she picked through the tiles for her seven.

"Now how would you know that?" her mother asked, pushing her brows together.

"Deborah writes to me, you know."

"Oh, you hadn't mentioned that. Now why would she let herself get pregnant so soon?"

"I guess it's *Gott*'s will," Martha said, lowering her voice.

"It's more likely, that it's Ebenezer's will," her grandmother added, clucking her tongue.

"Now, *Mamm*, you shouldn't talk like that in front of Martha. It ain't appropriate to discuss such things."

"She's a big *maed*, Sarah. I'm sure she knows the facts of life. After all, she's grown up on a farm."

"Well, still. I picked up a 'W.' So what letter did you get, *Mamm*?" she asked, changing the subject.

Martha took a long breath as she reached for her letter. She hated lying about anything. This would have to end someday. She would pray about it and try to find a way to be truthful, without losing the love of her life. Oh, why was life so complicated?

Daniel remained moody the next week or so, but since everyone in his family was prone to being quiet and remote, no one questioned his reason for being sullen. He was surprised the bishop hadn't come by again and hoped maybe the whole episode would just go away on its own and he could go on about his business.

He'd decided to pursue a relationship with that Molly girl he'd driven home a couple of times from the Singings. She wasn't as cute as Martha, but she seemed to like him and she knew when to keep her mouth shut. Martha was too opinionated and self-educated to suit him when it came right down to it. He had probably been more influenced by her appearance. She sure had beautiful brown eyes and a nice figure—what he could see of it anyway, with those loose frocks and aprons the Amish girls wore.

In the end though, it was more important to marry a woman who would know her place and not be argumentative or too opinionated. Hopefully, Molly was that woman. He wanted to settle down soon and have a family. *Jah*, he'd go to the next Singing, only this time he'd stop by her place first and make arrangements to pick her up as well as bring her home. Perhaps, he should go tonight after supper to ask her about going with him. He didn't want any other guys to beat him to it. He saw one of his friends talking to her and laughing at the last Sing. And hopefully, Martha would not be there to make things more awkward. She was probably mourning over her loss of that Paul character. Since her father had kicked them both out, he was sure that relationship was done. It would serve her right if she never had another beau, but he doubted that would happen with a looker like her.

After they had a supper of cold cuts and rolls, he took the open buggy and drove the half mile to Molly Zook's house. She was outside throwing a ball around with two of her younger brothers when he pulled in. She stopped when she realized it was him and went over to greet him.

"So how are you, Daniel? I haven't seen you at church services lately. Have you been sick?"

"Uh, a little. Busy, I guess with the harvest and all. I'll probably go next week."

"Want to play catch with us?"

"*Nee*. I'd rather take a walk with just you."

Her eyes widened and she grinned. "Okay." She turned towards her brothers and told them to go on without her. Daniel tethered his horse and then they walked over to the stable and patted the horses in their stalls.

"Going to the Singing this Sunday?" he asked.

"Probably." She kept her eyes focused on her driving horse. "Why do you ask?"

"Wanna go with me?"

"Sure."

"*Gut*. I'll pick you up around seven."

"Okay."

"You don't have to go with me, if you don't want to," he said, studying her expression.

"It's just I thought you were interested in Martha Troyer."

"*Nee.* I don't even like her anymore."

"Oh. Then I guess I should be glad you asked me. I know you could ask any girl you wanted."

"*Jah*? You think so?" he said, allowing a smile.

"*Jah*, you're popular."

"I never knew that."

"Well, not the *most* popular…"

He began to frown instead, but she looked over and grinned. "I'm teasing, Daniel."

"Oh," he said, wondering if she was going to be like Martha—always making jokes. He hoped not. He much preferred women who were serious-minded. Oh well, he'd give her a chance. After all, she was cute.

After about an hour, he made an excuse to leave. He went into the kitchen where her parents were having coffee and said good-bye to them as well. May as well make a good impression on the family, just in case he became serious. *Jah*, he knew what he was supposed to do, but sometimes it was too much of an effort. He'd be glad when he finally married and could just be himself—whatever that was.

Sunday, Daniel made up an excuse not to go to the church service. He claimed he had a migraine headache, though he'd never had one before. But when it was time to get ready for the Singing, he used the closed buggy and set out for Molly's home.

When he arrived, he had hoped she'd be waiting for him and he wouldn't have to take care of the buggy and make small talk with the family again. Since she wasn't visible, he looped the reins around the trunk of a tree by

the driveway and went up to the front door and knocked.
A few minutes later, Molly's father opened the door. He
placed his hands on his hips and glared at Daniel. "My
dochder ain't going with you. We don't want you coming by again."

"What's wrong? She agreed—"

"That was before we heard about you punching another man."

"Where did you hear about that?" Daniel could feel
himself perspire and he wiped his forehead with his arm,
removing his straw hat first.

"It don't matter. Is it true?"

"Well, you have to know all the facts."

"So, it is true. What kind of Amishman are you?"

"I haven't even been banned and already you treat
me like I'm guilty. That ain't right."

"You can leave now." He wrapped his arms and stood,
his legs slightly separated, daring Daniel to make another move or comment.

He turned and stomped toward his buggy. "I didn't
even throw the first punch!" he yelled back.

Herr Zook stood silently, barely moving a muscle.

As Daniel pulled away, he thought he heard Molly
crying in the background. It just wasn't fair to judge
a man without having all the facts. Chances were, the
bishop wouldn't even bring it up again.

Instead of attending the Sing, he returned to his home
and took his two-wheeler for a run. He needed to get the
frustration and anger out of his system. He sure didn't
feel real Amish this night. Just maybe he wasn't cut out
to be an Amishman.

Chapter Twenty-Seven

It was late October now and things were still up in the air about the confrontation between Paul and Daniel. So far, neither young man had been approached by their church leadership to make a public confession, but Daniel no longer attended church. Normally, someone in authority would have been around to reprimand him, but things were quiet, and he was pleased he wasn't being harassed.

He figured it would be difficult to get an Amish girl interested in him at this point if they heard about what happened, so he started going into town in the evenings to make friends with some of the English youth. There was a girl he was attracted to, but he decided to buy some regular English clothing at the local thrift shop before approaching her for a date.

Paul continued to attend his church back in Lewistown and though he hadn't been able to make the trip to Paradise to see Martha yet due to the heavy workload, they spoke every evening and continued to write each other frequently. He sent his letters through Naomi, who was still at her cousin's house since her mother had the help she needed back home.

Another week passed. Finally, he and Martha made arrangements for him to come the next day, Saturday afternoon, and remain until Sunday, since the service was to be held at one of the homes and they'd have some time together alone on Sunday while the congregation celebrated one of the elder's birthdays after the service, keeping the family away longer than normal.

It meant that Martha would have to make up a lie about feeling ill so she could remain behind. Unfortunately, she was getting used to living a lie and it no longer made her feel as guilty, which in itself was troubling. She rationalized that she was only doing so to keep her parents from being distressed about her intent to one day marry a man they objected to. She still attempted to change her father's mind about allowing Paul to pay a visit. He no longer made it sound like an impossibility, but he had not yet accepted the idea. She continued to pray for a softening of his heart.

Even though Saturday, Paul would spend his time alone, he enjoyed checking out the area. Martha wondered if he was thinking about moving there when the time came.

That Friday night, the bishop and one of the elders appeared at the Troyer's back door. Elder Samuel had a grim expression on his face and Martha wondered if someone had died. She led the two men into the kitchen and called her parents who were seated in the sitting room. When they came into the kitchen, they greeted their visitors. Martha was about to leave when Bishop

Josiah held up his hand. "This involves you, Martha. You can stay."

She remained standing, as did the other adults.

The bishop coughed into his hand and then cleared his throat. "I wanted you to be the first to hear. We've been to the Beilers' house this week to discuss the events that took place here at your home between those two young Amishmen. We've talked at length with their *sohn*, Daniel, about his sinful behavior, and we've asked him to make a sincere repentance in accordance with the rules of the *Ordnung* and ask *Gott* for forgiveness. So far, he has refused to do so, and if that attitude continues, we'll have no alternative but to have him excommunicated. He will be shunned as is appropriate and unless he has a change of heart, we will not consider him part of our Amish community. We'll give him one more chance to repent, though. That's our main goal, since he is still one of us. Though we must forgive, we can't allow such behavior to go on unchecked."

"Wow," Martha said softly. Bishop Josiah turned to her, scowling. "We have also been in touch with the other Amishman involved—at least with his bishop. I expect they will be addressing the situation very soon. I understand you have no contact with him anymore. Am I correct?"

Oh no! Martha had no idea such a question would be asked. She stood gaping at the man, feeling the eyes of all the adults on her. She knew her parents were waiting for her to respond in the negative. But to lie to a bishop? A man appointed by *Gott*? How could she possibly put herself in such a position?

"I... I haven't seen him in quite a while," she began.

"And you have no correspondence with him?" Bishop

Josiah asked, pulling now on his beard, as he zeroed in on her eyes with his dark direct stare.

"She's a *gut* girl," her mother started.

"Hush. Let the *maed* answer for herself," Melvin said abruptly. "Tell him, Martha."

"Oh, dear," she said, breaking down into a torrent of tears. "We...write...once in a while."

"Oh my," she heard her mother whisper, close to tears herself. Her father remained silent.

"You are to stop any communication with this man at once—at least until I hear from his bishop as to his decision. If he goes before his congregation and makes a full confession of his sins and vows to never lay a hand on another person again in anger, then he will be considered forgiven and will remain in his Amish community. Do you understand?"

She was unable to speak, even though she had controlled her tears to some degree. She nodded her head, without looking up."

"Look me in the eye, Martha."

She wiped her eyes with her sleeve and lifted her chin, placing her focus on him. "I understand."

"There will be no communication until I have heard back and know what has transpired. Do you promise?"

"I guess."

"That's not what I expect to hear," he said, his voice steady and somber.

"I'll try."

"Martha, what are you doing?" her father broke in. "Tell the bishop you won't disobey him. This is serious."

"I know, but... I love him so much." She started weeping all over again.

The bishop looked over at her father. "You don't have

much control over this *maed*. I'll leave it in your hands now to see that she is obedient, or it will be necessary for some serious correction. I hope you can make her understand the severity of this."

"*Jah*, Bishop, I will. She'll be fine. She's just upset, but she's a *gut* girl. Never given us a moment's problem."

The bishop replaced his hat and turned to leave with the elder walking behind him. "I'll get back to you when I have any further information to relay to you." They closed the door behind them.

Martha sat on a kitchen chair and laid her head on the table, continuing to cry. She felt her mother's hand pat her shoulder. "Now, Martha, stop this crying now. It ain't the end of the world."

Her father remained silent, but she could feel his presence and she feared looking up at him. Then she heard him leave the room and trudge up the stairs.

"Oh *Mamm*, what am I to do? Paul's coming to see me. We haven't seen each other since—like forever."

"Shame, shame." Her mother withdrew her hand. "I can't believe you'd be so disobedient. We've always trusted you. You've been lying right along to us. I'm shocked."

"Oh, I didn't want to lie to you. I love you so much, but I also love Paul and I can't break up with him. I can't! We want to marry and live right and stay Amish and be near you and give you lots of *grossboppli*. Please try to understand. Just for a moment's mistake, should our whole lives be ruined?"

"Oh Martha," her mother said as she took a seat across from her. "I don't know what to say. You know how your father feels."

"He could give Paul a chance. Especially if he's

willing to ask forgiveness and make a vow to never do it again. He should be allowed a second chance. *Gott* would want that. We're to forgive. Why is that so hard to do all of a sudden?"

"I'm sure if Paul did all that, your *daed* and I would be willing to meet with him. But you don't know if he'd repent. He might just leave the Amish and then what? Would you break our hearts and leave us as well?" Now tears streamed down Sarah's face.

"*Nee*, I could never hurt you like that."

"You'd give Paul up for us?"

"I'd try."

"Martha, that's not sounding too *gut*. I don't think you would give him up."

"I'd want to, but I don't want to add another lie. I'm just not sure I could. Please understand. Please."

"I can't speak any more about this. I'm going up to try to comfort your *daed*. You must pray about all this and do the right thing. You were raised to be honorable. What you've done is disgraceful, but you can make amends. Think hard about your choices."

Sarah rose and slowly went up the staircase to talk to her husband. She had no idea what to say. She knew one thing though. She loved her daughter with all her heart, and even if she were shunned, she'd go right on loving her, till death drove them apart.

Chapter Twenty-Eight

Martha went to her room and laid on her bed. She needed to calm down before calling Paul. He'd have to stay back in Lewistown for now. She couldn't get in more trouble or have him complicate his life any more than it was. What a nightmare. Her parents were such honorable people. They'd never do anything so deceptive. How much shame they must feel having her for a daughter. They probably wished she'd never been born. The guilt nearly overwhelmed her.

Once she felt stable enough to call, she reached for her phone and turned it on. Nothing! No charge! She hadn't checked the amount of charge she had remaining for the last several days. How careless of her. How could she get in touch with him now? He would be heading over to Paradise the next day. She couldn't leave the house now. Her father would never let her out this late and the next morning her *Aenti* Lizzy was having her and her mother and grandmother over for a special lunch since her husband was going overnight to visit with his elder brother, who was recuperating from surgery. They were probably going to work on the quilt after the meal. She'd have no opportunity to get to the library.

With everything that was happening, and the lack of trust now between her and her parents, they wouldn't leave her alone on Sunday. What could she do? Somehow, she'd have to try to get her phone re-charged before Paul left for Paradise, though he had planned to leave early and do some hiking and exploring first.

Martha realized she hadn't finished cleaning up the kitchen from supper. She didn't want her parents to become any more upset with her than they were already, so she made her way downstairs to dry the dishes and put them away. Her grandparents were sitting in the living room with her mother and father. When they saw her enter the room, her *mammi* shook her head. "Martha, how could you?"

Her grandfather leaned back in the armchair and folded his arms. He had no smile for her this night. Her father stood, walked over to the front window and stared out, his body slumped forward as if weak from age. She had done this to her family. In her mind, all she had done was fall in love and the rest had just fallen into place, ruining their future together.

"I'm so sorry I've hurt you all," she said weakly. "I never meant to."

"*Jah*, but once a lie starts, it multiplies into many," her grandmother replied, her voice filled with sorrow.

"I came down to finish the kitchen," Martha said softly, moving towards the hallway to the back.

"It's all right. I already redded up," her mother said.

"You can go up to your room, Martha," her father said, still staring out the window into the darkness of the evening.

She turned and left without another word. What was there to say? There was no possibility of Paul becoming part of the family now. They were both disgraced. Liars. Deceitful liars.

It was impossible to sleep. She tossed about, trying to pray, but no words formed. Had *Gott* turned his back on her as well?

The next morning, she went downstairs earlier than usual to start breakfast for her father, who was still upstairs dressing. She put on the coffee and fried up several pieces of scrapple in a frying pan. Then she set his place, putting his favorite mug by his spoon. Her hand shook slightly when she heard his footsteps on the stairs.

"*Gude mariye*," she said softly. He returned the greeting, and she was surprised that his voice sounded almost normal.

"I'll have your *kaffi* ready soon, *Daed*."

"*Jah*. It smells *gut*." He reached for the morning paper, which she had brought in from the yard, and sat down at his place.

As she turned the scrapple, he cleared his throat. "Your *mamm* said to get ready to go to your *aenti*'s house. You'll have your breakfast over there today."

The shock of these events almost made her drop the spatula. She'd been forgiven, that easily? "Okay," she managed to say. She wanted to look at his expression to see if they matched his casual voice, but she couldn't bring herself to take the chance that it might be disappointing.

"Well, I'll be," he began referring to something on the front page. "The auction is being postponed due to rain this afternoon. What's a little mud at a mud sale?" he asked, amused at his own joke.

Martha laughed, though it was somewhat forced. "That's a *gut* one, *Daed*."

"*Jah*," he said, nodding.

"I was going to take your *dawdi* to the sale, but no point now, if there ain't one."

"Will it be next week?"

"*Jah*, hopefully. Maybe you'd like to go with us."

"Maybe," she said, feeling suddenly light on her feet. Oh, how she loved her *daed*.

After serving him three over-light eggs along with the scrapple and rye toast, she wiped down the stove. He went out to the barn and she ran upstairs and dressed in one of her prettiest blue outfits. Life would go on, though the thought of Paul arriving at the house the next day and finding her gone, left a horrible pit in her stomach. She intended to take her phone with her in case she found a way to re-charge it, but in her hurry, she accidentally left it on the top of her dresser.

Her mother was already dressed and waiting for her when she got downstairs, and without further discussion, they walked over to the *dawdi-haus* and knocked for *Mammi*, who came out with a large bag of material along with the directions for the quilt. What a shame there'd be no wedding in this family. Probably not for a long, long time.

Apparently, while Martha and her grandmother were cutting some of the pointed pieces for the quilt, her mother filled her aunt in on the details of the day before. She was rather subdued after that and Martha felt the pain of hurting yet another of her loved ones. While everyone made an effort to appear normal, there was a pall over the whole day. It was a relief when her mother finally decided it was time to go back home.

When they got back, Martha and her mother went into the basement and removed the dry towels and some underwear, which they'd hung up earlier on the long lines which stretched from one end of the sprawling dirt-floored basement to the other.

There was a second load of sheets waiting to be hung.

"I'll take these upstairs, Martha, if you can hang the sheets for me."

"Sure. Then should I start supper?"

"You can. We have leftover frankfurters and baked beans. Just heat them up. Your *daed* wants to eat by five."

Sarah lugged the fresh towels and clothing upstairs and placed the towels and washcloths back in the bathroom linen closet. Then she took a nightgown and several pairs of Martha's panties into her daughter's room, preparing to place them in one of the drawers. Something unfamiliar caught her eye. She gasped as she realized it was one of those cell phones she'd seen the English carry around with them—in Martha's room. On her dresser! It could only mean one thing. Another betrayal. Her heart sank and her legs felt wobbly. She sat down on the edge of Martha's bed and stared at the black phone. Her daughter was moving into another world and there was little she could do to stop her. She rose and slipped the phone into her apron pocket and went back downstairs.

On Saturday, Paul arrived in the area around four-thirty. It was raining too hard to go for any kind of hike, so he found a small coffee shop and purchased a magazine about carpentry and after trying unsuccess-fully once more to reach Martha, he dialed a rooming house he'd learned about and rented a room for the night. Around six, the rain stopped and he made his way to a small grocery store and purchased a pre-packaged ham sandwich to take with him to the rooming house for his supper.

He was the only one staying there, so the bathroom, which was shared by three guestrooms, was his exclu-sively. The elderly couple who ran the home, were pleas-ant, but left him pretty much to himself. There was no lock on his bedroom door, but he didn't feel it necessary to have one.

He read until midnight and then slept soundly, even though he was excited about seeing Martha the next day. It had been too long.

Chapter Twenty-Nine

Martha would make one attempt to convince her parents she was too ill to attend the church service. She mussed her hair up and placed a light robe over her nightgown before heading downstairs. Her parents were seated at the table, eating oatmeal when she arrived. They'd obviously been talking about her, since as she approached the kitchen, she heard her mother hush her father. "Not now," was all she could make out.

They greeted each other, though there was a strain in the words.

"I'm sorry, but I don't think I can make it to the service today," Martha started saying.

"You'll make it." Her father's tone left little doubt about the outcome.

"But *Daed*, I'm feeling like I'm coming down with a fever."

"No more lies, *dochder*," he added as he took another spoonful of cereal, staring down at his bowl.

She heard her mother's voice choke up as she asked him to pass the sugar bowl.

"Well, I sure don't want to make any of the *kinner*

sick," Martha added as her final attempt. Her heart was beating rapidly and she had little appetite for cereal.

"You'd better get dressed," her mother said, concentrating on sprinkling a teaspoon of sugar over her oatmeal. "We want to get started in twenty minutes."

"Okay." Martha walked slowly up the stairs. When she reached her dresser to find clean underwear, she visualized how she'd left the room the day before. Her heart sank when she couldn't recall re-placing the phone in the drawer. She checked under the clothing. No phone. Then she remembered her mother coming up to leave off the clean clothes.

Oh, mercy, she'd found the phone! No wonder they were acting the way they were. Why didn't they confront her? She figured then that they'd wait until after church service. Maybe even wait until the next day. At least the phone wasn't working so they wouldn't be able to call Paul. They probably figured out he was headed there since she'd tried to get out of attending the service. Goodness! That surely wouldn't help the situation. Oh, how a lie could end up complicating her whole life.

To hide a lie, a thousand lies are needed.

Around ten, Paul made his way by foot over to Martha's home. With each step, he became more excited. He couldn't wait to hold her in his arms and smell her lovely clean Ivory soap skin and hear her gentle voice.

When he saw the buggy was missing, he was confident that she was waiting there alone—for him. He knocked gently at first at the kitchen door. When he peered inside through the door window, he noticed it was dark. No welcoming kerosene lamp this time. There were no homemade buns on the table. The coffee pot was not perking.

Everything spoke of an empty house, but surely...

He knocked harder this time and then shouted through the glass pane. Nothing. Was she ill? Should he break in? Her parents would never have left her alone, if she'd truly been sick. No, she had most likely gone with them. In her last letter, she had sounded so cheerful, excited about their upcoming visit.

He sat on the back stoop and took off his hat. He twisted it in circles, wondering what he could do. Should he wait for their return? Had her parents reconciled with her about giving him a chance? He stood and walked around the property. It was muddy from all the rain that had fallen on Saturday and he left tracks on the drive. He went over to the barn and looked inside. Maybe she was milking the cows. One of their cows looked up at him as she chewed her cud. Everything was tidy. Nothing amiss.

After walking around for about an hour, he decided to call his ride and have him pick him up back at the place where he spent the night. The driver sounded surprised to be returning this soon, but Paul gave no explanation. He had none. He still had time to put in, since it would be a couple hours before his ride arrived, so he went back to the rooming house and waited there. He asked for paper and pen from the owner and wrote a short note, which he decided to leave off at Martha's house on the way home. It wouldn't be out of his way more than half a mile. He'd leave it in her mailbox, since she'd told him she always picked up the mail for the whole family. That had been her job since she was five years old and no one daresn't beat her to it. It was quite the family joke.

After he wrote it, he read it over.

Dear Martha,
I'm so disappointed to find you not at home. I figure your phone lost its charge since you didn't call me, and that isn't like you. At first I was afraid you were too sick to answer the door, but then I knew your parents wouldn't leave you alone if you were really sick.

I hope you aren't in any trouble. I would hate to think I was the cause of any misunderstanding you had with your parents. I know how much you love them. Even though I love you with all my heart and want us to be married one day, I would never do anything to hurt your relationship with them. You would never be happy if that happened. Please let me know why you weren't home.

Things are getting even busier at the shop. I think people are thinking about Christmas already, so I don't know when I can get away again. Please call me when your phone is working again. I hope it didn't get broken.

I love you, dear Martha.
Paul

Eventually, he heard Skip Davis pull up to the house. He paid the couple for the night's stay and took his overnight bag to the car, placing it on the floor of the back seat. Then he asked Skip to drive by Martha's house so he could drop off the letter. When they arrived, he could see the buggy parked in the back. He told the driver to drive farther up the road before stopping. Then he walked back to the mailbox and placed it deep inside, without flagging it. When he looked up at the house, he thought he saw Martha silhouetted by a soft lamp up at her bedroom window. He lifted a hand, but the light went out and he wondered if he'd only imagined her being there. His heart was heavy as he returned to the waiting car. Would he ever see her again?

Martha drew back from her window. Tears flowed until she could barely breathe. She knew he'd left something for her in the mailbox. After everyone was down for the night, she'd have to go retrieve it. Hopefully, he wasn't angry with her. She couldn't bear anyone else being upset with her. She sure was making a botched job of her life. Maybe she should just leave for a while until she sorted everything out in her mind. She found herself upset with the whole Amish lifestyle at this point. Why was it so wrong to own a phone, or have electricity, for heaven's sake?

Maybe her friend, Naomi, had the right idea. She seemed serious about testing the waters of the English world. If it weren't for Paul, Martha might seriously consider doing the same, but as long as she and Paul were serious about each other, she wouldn't consider leaving, at least permanently.

It seemed to take hours before her parents were settled down for the night. Just to be sure, she checked to see if there was light coming from under their bedroom door. It was black and she could hear light snores coming from her father as she tiptoed past their door, carrying her own lantern for light.

It was chilly out and she pulled her woolen cape closely around her shoulders as she walked up to the front of the drive. Fortunately, the moon was nearly full, so she was able to see her way clearly up to the mailbox where she removed the folded paper. There was no envelope, so it was a good thing she had retrieved it before anyone else might have opened it.

She tucked it in to her robe and made her way back to her room, where she had placed the lamp before going outside. She raised the wick enough to be able to read his writing. After reading it, she re-read it. It was not reassuring to her. He sounded too ready to back away if they continued to meet opposition to their relationship. She knew he still loved her, but perhaps not enough to put up with all this hostility coming from her family. They really hadn't given him a chance to explain himself. It wasn't fair. Perhaps, they feared she'd move away if they encouraged them to marry, and perhaps she would, but don't you want your children to be happy? It's not like she'd be moving out of state, for heaven's sake. It was merely a two-hour drive. It seemed a wee bit selfish for them to make a big deal out of such a minor obstacle. Granted, they wouldn't see each other every weekend, but she knew English families who lived hundreds of miles from their married children and somehow, they survived.

She still shivered from being outside, but she placed a second quilt over her bed and crawled beneath. He hadn't mentioned anything about his bishop paying him a visit. She wondered if he just didn't want to upset her, or if his district didn't take it as seriously somehow. Either way, it was just a matter of time before he'd be confronted. What would his decision be? Surely, he'd vow to follow the rules of the church and confess his sinful behavior, unlike Daniel, who was too proud and arrogant to admit to being wrong.

The next day passed slowly. Her mother barely spoke to her and her father didn't even say good morning. It was the phone, she was sure and certain of that. Things had been improving before her mother found it. How could she have been so careless?

After the myriad chores were done, she asked her mother if she could use the buggy to visit Naomi, who was supposed to be back home by now.

"You'll have to ask your *daed*," she answered, searching through her sewing box for scissors.

"Is he outside?"

"*Jah*. Grooming the horses."

"But it's okay with you?"

"I don't care one way or the other."

Her father nodded when she asked, without adding a comment. Normally, he would have harnessed Chessy to the buggy for her, but he continued brushing down their other horse without offering another word.

It would be good to get away, even if it was just a couple of hours. The strain was affecting her physically as well as mentally.

When she arrived at Naomi's, her two younger brothers, Tommy and Bruce, were turning over part of the vegetable garden, preparing it for the following season. They barely looked up and she saw Naomi pushing Patty in her carriage, the child most unhappy—crying vigorously. Naomi looked up with a mix of frustration and pleasure when she saw it was her friend.

"Martha, I was hoping you were coming by today. Patty is acting like a bear. Nothing pleases her. I wish I was back with my cousin, Valerie. I had so much fun, Martha. We even went to parties. Her parents let her do anything, just about."

"Do you want me to hold Patty for a while for you? Maybe she needs to be bounced a little."

"You can try. It's her teeth coming through. Her gums are all puffy." Naomi reached in the carriage and picked up her sister. Before handing her over, she held her over her shoulder and patted her back while humming a tune. The baby quieted down, so she held on to her and they walked together around the property.

"You look like you didn't sleep last night," Naomi said, looking closely at her friend.

"I got about three hours' sleep, is all." Then she told Naomi everything that had transpired.

Naomi shook her head. "That's awful. You poor thing. Maybe you need to get away for a while and let everyone cool off. It's hard to live under that much tension."

"*Jah*, you said that right. My stomach is so messed up—I feel like I could *kutz*."

"Listen, I'm serious about leaving here. Mom doesn't really need me that much and we've never gotten along very *gut*. *Daed* never sticks up for me. I've had it. Valerie told me about a small apartment in their neighborhood that's empty. She even knows the owner and it's cheap. If we both got jobs and put our money together, we could afford to live there. It would be fun! What do you think?"

"I… I never even thought about actually leaving, but if it was just temporary and my parents understood, they'd probably be glad to have me gone for a while, too. They barely speak to me."

"Would they give you your phone back?"

"I have no idea."

"Do you have any money saved?" Naomi patted Patty though she'd already fallen asleep.

"Only about three hundred dollars. I've been saving forever."

"I have almost five hundred, so we could pay the rent for the first month. It's only four hundred. They'd probably waive the security."

"What's security?" Martha asked.

"Oh, something they hold on to in case you wreck the place, but I told you, Valerie knows the people. They'd give her a break, I'm sure."

"What would my parents say?" Martha asked, more to herself than to her friend.

"Oh, they'd probably be mad at first, but you never did anything for your *Rumspringa*, so they'd probably let you go. They know me and my family. It's not like you'd be living with a guy or something."

"True, but they might think I was lying again and moving in with Paul. They don't trust me at all. That's one of the worst parts of all this. They're such honest people—they'd never tell me a lie."

"Think about it. The apartment just came up for rent, but it won't last long because it's cheap and in a nice neighborhood. I saw it from the outside."

"Does it have two bedrooms?" Martha asked.

"Just one, but it's already furnished and there's a pull-out sofa in the living room. No dishwasher, but like who cares? It has electricity!"

"And television?"

"*Nee*. But if we make enough money, we could buy one later."

"What would we do? Who'd even hire us?"

"We sure know how to baby-sit, and we could learn to waitress or clean houses or anything. It's not like we have no skills at all."

"True. Gosh, I'm actually kind of excited about the idea. Let me think about it. How far is it from here?"

"About an hour by car. Half way between Paradise and Lewistown."

"Oh, my goodness! I'd be closer to Paul. If my parents find that out, they'll have a fit."

"Don't mention it. They probably wouldn't figure it out. After all, if they're like my parents, they don't travel much."

"True, but if they ask…"

"I bet they won't. Let me put Patty down. She's finally asleep and I could use a glass of iced tea. What about you?"

"Sounds *gut*. I didn't eat breakfast."

"Then I'll give you some lemon sponge pie to go with it. My *aenti* brought it over earlier. See? My *mamm* has lots of people to help her out. She could easily do it without me."

"And my *mudder* has no other *kinner*. Of course, she does help out with her parents."

"But she doesn't need you, that's the thing. So now's the time to spread your wings."

Martha felt some hope for the first time in quite a while. She'd be on her own, earning her own money, making her own decisions, and best of all—she'd be an hour closer to Paul!

Chapter Thirty

It took several days for Martha to find the courage to discuss her possible plans to move out of the house and live on her own. Her parents were actually making it easier for her by their rejection of her. She caught her mother with tears in her eyes more than once, but if she went over to touch her arm or show affection, Sarah would pull away and avoid her. It was awful to live in that cold atmosphere, especially when she'd been used to such a loving home. It was difficult for her to understand their actions. Certainly, if she had a child someday, she'd never treat them like this.

The morning she decided to brave the discussion, she had received a warmer letter from Paul. He mentioned that someone from his congregation had stopped by to talk to him about the episode with Daniel. While the elder hadn't been insistent about Paul making a confession of his sin and repenting, Paul told Martha he thought if the man returned, he would offer to do just that. Probably, the elder was giving him a chance to come forward on his own before applying any pressure. Martha was relieved to know Paul was willing to step forward on his own. She also knew he did consider what he'd done a sin, and it would help him to make his confession.

She had written about Daniel and his refusal to admit his error. What a difference in the two men. Thank God, she hadn't committed herself to Daniel. What a disaster that would have been. Maybe once her parents found out Paul had made his confession, they'd be more willing to meet with him. Surely, they'd be able to see the difference between the two men. Martha wondered if her parents, who had not been that enamored of Daniel, were just hoping she'd settle for him and live right next door. That possibility seemed a little selfish, she had to admit.

After supper, her grandparents joined them in the sitting room for devotions. They came over nearly every evening and had supper with them and then stayed on for the Bible reading. It was usually a very pleasant time, but as of late, it felt awkward. Martha decided to bring up the idea of moving out, while her grandparents were still there, since she might get support from her *mammi*, who usually tried to see things through her granddaughter's eyes.

Her father finished reading from Isaiah and set the Bible in its wooden box. Then he was about to reach for the latest newspaper, when Martha asked if she could speak to everyone about something she felt important. Her mother and grandmother had been about to do a crossword puzzle together, but everyone stopped to listen.

Martha cleared her voice. "I have been thinking about something for a while now and I believe I've made up my mind after giving it much thought. I'm afraid you may not like the idea right away, but in the end, I believe you'll all agree it is for the best."

"Get on with it *dochder*," Melvin said, placing the folded paper on the floor.

"Well, as you know, my friend Naomi just returned from a visit with her cousin. While she was there, she saw a really nice apartment for rent. Well, she didn't go inside it, but she liked the way it looked on the outside so—"

"We don't need all the details. Continue," her father stated, wrapping his arms in front of his chest. She noticed her grandfather sat back in his chair and pulled on his suspenders with his thumbs. One of his signs of concentration, she'd discovered. The women remained silent and focused on her every word.

"Well, anyway, Naomi wants to rent the apartment and she'd like me to be her roommate."

"And where exactly is this wonderful apartment?" her father asked.

"I'm not sure of the name of the town, but it's not far away."

"How far away?" her grandfather asked.

"It's only about an hour's drive."

"With a buggy or a car?" her grandmother asked.

"That's with a car, I guess."

"In other words, it's too far for us to visit with our buggy," her father added.

"But it's easy to get a driver…"

Sarah, who hadn't said a word, began speaking, her voice quivering. "Why do you want to get away from your family?"

"It's not that, *Mamm*. I'm at an age where I need to think about my future."

"Seems to me, you could think about it right here…in

your home with your family," her father said, his voice slightly elevated.

"It's not the same. Besides, everyone is always mad at me now, and it's making my stomach all upset. I can't take it anymore. I feel like no one really cares about me just because of a stupid fight that was over in less than a minute!" She could no longer hold back her tears, but she wouldn't allow her voice to waver. She had to remain strong.

"Of course, we all care about you," her mother said, "but I'd be lying if I told you I wasn't disappointed in you. We've always trusted you, Martha, but sometimes I feel we don't even know who you are anymore."

"I haven't changed. It's still me. The only difference is I'm in love and you won't even meet with him. You won't give him a chance and it's breaking my heart."

"He behaved very badly," her father said. "We want what's best for you. Not a husband whose temper can't be trusted."

"You don't understand. Daniel pushed him to it. It was all his fault and Paul will repent and kneel before anyone and everyone admitting his sin. You don't see Daniel do that. No, he's too proud and doesn't think he ever does anything wrong and you wanted me to marry him. I can't imagine what my life would have been like if I had married him."

"You acted like you loved him for a while. We didn't push you into anything," her father said.

"But when I tried to end it, you kept on pushing me."

"We want to have you live by us. Be part of our lives. Is that so wrong?" Sarah asked.

"If you don't look at what it would do to me—*jah*. It seems you didn't care how I felt about him as long as I lived nearby. That's selfish."

"Martha, apologize to your *mudder*. She doesn't have a selfish bone in her body."

"I am sorry I have to say these things. You can see now why I need to get away for a while and do some thinking. Everything seems to be a mess in my life right now. It probably would only be for a short time."

"Are you sure you're not planning on living with that Paul?"

"*Daed*! How could you think that? Unmarrried? That would never happen. You don't know me at all!"

"I'm sorry, it's just that the English seem to think there's nothing wrong with it and I don't know if you want to leave the Amish and this is your way of breaking bonds with us," he said, lowering his head. He took a seat on the sofa next to Sarah and took her hand in his. "What do you think, Sarah? Should we let our little *maed* try her wings?"

Sarah leaned her head against his chest. "It seems so wrong. I'm so afraid we'll lose our *dochder*."

"*Nee*, I will always love you," Martha said forcefully. "You have to know that. No matter where I live, who I marry, nothing can change my love for you. You're the best family in the whole wide world, but I'm so confused right now. Just let me go for a while. I'll get a job and support myself. I won't be a burden to you in any way and I promise I'll visit often."

Sarah sat apart from her husband, but held onto his hand. She reached out for Martha with her other arm and Martha sat next to her and embraced her. She then patted her father's shoulder. Her grandparents were silent, their emotions close to the surface. Martha then went over to each of them and kissed them on the cheeks. "Please understand."

"*Jah*, I was young once, Martha," her grandmother said softly. "You'll be back little one. The world is large and lonely. Just be careful not to fall into their ways out there. Always hold true to your values and stay close to *Gott* and He'll protect you."

Martha nodded, unable to speak any further. The tears kept flowing.

"Your *mamm* and I will talk to you about it tomorrow, Martha. I think we all need to sleep on it."

"And pray about it," Sarah added.

"*Jah*. I'll go up now. *Gut nacht*, everyone," she added as she made her way up the stairs.

As she laid in bed, she left the kerosene lamp on low and looked around as it cast shadows against her wall. This was the only room she'd ever known. It spoke of love, growing from child to adult, going through the traumas every young person faces: the disappointments, the joys, many birthday celebrations, the tears and illnesses. It was all right here in this simple ten-foot square room with its white walls and simple furnishings, yet it spoke to her of security and love. Was she ready to leave all this for the unknown? Why did she even feel the need to be on her own?

Perhaps, she should have given it more thought before making the announcement tonight. Another day or two and maybe things would have seemed so different. But what was done, was done. She would break her strong ties—at least temporarily—and discover exactly who she was. She just hoped in the end, she would like the young woman she had become.

* * * * *

"There won't be another bus going that way until the day after tomorrow."

"Are you sure?" Gemma Lapp stared at the agent behind the counter in stunned disbelief.

"Of course I'm sure. I work for the bus company."

She clasped her hands together tightly, praying the tears that pricked the backs of her eyes wouldn't start flowing. She couldn't afford a motel room for two nights.

She wheeled her suitcase over to the bench. Sitting down with a sigh, she moved her suitcase in front of her so she could prop up her swollen feet. After two solid days on a bus she was ready to lie down. Anywhere.

She bit her lower lip to stop it from quivering. She could place a call to the phone shack her parents shared with their Amish neighbors to let them know she was returning and ask her father to send a car for her, but she would have to leave a message.

Any message she left would be overheard. If she gave the real reason, even Jesse Crump would know before she reached home. She couldn't bear that, although she didn't understand why his opinion mattered so much. His stoic face wouldn't reveal his thoughts, but he was sure to gloat when he learned he'd been right about her reckless ways. He had said she was looking for trouble and that she would find it sooner or later. Well, she had found it all right.

No, she wouldn't call. What she had to say was better said face-to-face. She was cowardly enough to delay as long as possible.

She didn't know how she was going to find the courage to tell her mother and father that she was six months pregnant, and Robert Troyer, the man who'd promised to marry her, was long gone.

Don't miss
Shelter from the Storm *by* USA TODAY
bestselling author Patricia Davids,
available September 2019 wherever
Love Inspired® books and ebooks are sold.

www.LoveInspired.com

*Could a pretend Christmastime courtship
lead to a forever match?*

Read on for a sneak preview of
Her Amish Holiday Suitor, *part of Carrie Lighte's
Amish Country Courtships miniseries.*

Nick took his seat next to her and picked up the reins,
but before moving onward, he said, "I don't understand it,
Lucy. Why is my caring about you such an awful thing?"
His voice was quivering and Lucy felt a pang of guilt. She
knew she was overreacting. Rather, she was reacting to
a heartache that had plagued her for years, not one Nick
had caused that evening.

"I don't expect you to understand," she said, wiping
her rough woolen mitten across her cheeks.

"But I want to. Can't you explain it to me?"

Nick's voice was so forlorn Lucy let her defenses drop.
"I've always been treated like this, my entire life. *Lucy's
too weak, too fragile, too small, she can't go outside or
run around or have any fun because she'll get sick. She'll
stop breathing. She'll wind up in the hospital.* My whole
life, Nick. And then the one little taste of utter abandon I
ever experienced—charging through the dark with a frosty
wind whisking against my face, feeling totally invigorated
and alive… You want to take that away from me, too."

She was crying so hard her words were barely
intelligible, but Nick didn't interrupt or attempt to quiet
her. When she finally settled down and could speak

normally again, she sniffed and asked, "May I use your handkerchief, please?"

"Sorry, I don't have one," Nick said. "But here, you can use my scarf. I don't mind."

The offer to use Nick's scarf to dry her eyes and blow her nose was so ridiculous and sweet all at once it caused Lucy to chuckle. "*Neh*, that's okay," she said, removing her mittens to dab her eyes with her bare fingers.

"I really am sorry," he repeated.

Lucy was embarrassed. "That's all right. I've stopped blubbering. I don't need a handkerchief after all."

"*Neh*, I mean I'm sorry I treated you in a way that made you feel…the way you feel. I didn't mean to. I was concerned. I care about you and I wouldn't want anything to happen to you. I especially wouldn't want to play a role in hurting you."

Lucy was overwhelmed by his words. No man had ever said anything like that to her before, even in friendship. "It's not your fault," she said. "And I do appreciate that you care. But I'm not as fragile as you think I am."

"Fragile? You? I don't think you're fragile at all, even if you are prone to pneumonia." Nick scoffed. "I think you're one of the most resilient women I've ever known."

Lucy was overwhelmed again. If this kept up, she was going to fall hard for Nick Burkholder. Maybe she already had.

Don't miss
Her Amish Holiday Suitor *by Carrie Lighte,*
available October 2019 wherever
Love Inspired® books and ebooks are sold.

Copyright © 2019 by Carrie Lighte

LIEXP0919

Love Inspired®

Discover wholesome and uplifting stories of faith, forgiveness and hope.

Join our social communities to connect with other readers who share your love!

Sign up for the Love Inspired newsletter at **LoveInspired.com** to be the first to find out about upcoming titles, special promotions and exclusive content.

CONNECT WITH US AT:

Facebook.com/groups/HarlequinConnection

 Facebook.com/LoveInspiredBooks

 Twitter.com/LoveInspiredBks

LISOCIAL2019

WE HOPE YOU ENJOYED THIS BOOK!

Love Inspired® SUSPENSE

Uncover the truth in these thrilling stories of faith in the face of crime from Love Inspired Suspense. Discover six new books available every month, wherever books are sold!

Reward the book lover in you!

Earn points on your purchase of new Harlequin books from participating retailers.

Turn your points into **FREE BOOKS** of your choice!

Join for FREE today at
www.HarlequinMyRewards.com.

Harlequin My Rewards is a free program (no fees) without any commitments or obligations.

MYR18